$\mathcal{A}$long with all the other visitors, B and George pressed closer, eager for a glimpse of the first candies to come out of the machine. No one spoke. Everyone seemed paused, poised on tiptoe for the unveiling of the first Fabulous Fruit.

There was a loud bang.

Like popping corn, one by one, the lights went out. The room was plunged into total darkness.

DISCOVER ALL THE MAGIC!

B Magical

The Chocolate Meltdown

By Lexi Connor

SCHOLASTIC INC.

New York   Toronto   London   Auckland
Sydney   Mexico City   New Delhi   Hong Kong

Special thanks to Julie Berry

ISBN 978-0-545-11740-1

12 11 10 9 8 7 6 5 4 3 2 1   10 11 12 13 14 15/0

Printed in the U.S.A.   40
First printing, October 2010

To Phil

Chapter 1

"Pinch me, B."

Beatrix Cicely, called B for short, looked in surprise at her best friend, George, who had pulled back his sleeve and thrust his arm out in front of her.

"Seriously. Pinch me! I must be dreaming. There's no other possible explanation for today."

B gave George's arm a harmless pinch. "Don't be silly, George! I told you that sooner or later, my dad would let you have a tour of Enchanted Chocolates. It was just a matter of time."

B and George both knew what few others in the world did — that Enchanted Chocolates candies were made by witches. Of course, they couldn't concoct spells and potions to make the chocolate — that would be cheating. They measured and mixed it the old-fashioned way. But, all the same, you couldn't have so many witches under the same roof without a little magic in the air. Maybe some of it did rub off on the chocolates — they *were* the world's best.

George wasn't a witch, and nonwitches were never supposed to know about magic, but he had long ago stumbled upon B's secret. And B's magic was unique. While most other witches formed spells with rhyming couplets, B made spells by spelling words.

George leaned back in Mr. Cicely's office chair and spun around. He inhaled, long and deep. "Just smell that chocolate!" He sat up and pointed at B. "I'll bet I buy more Enchanted Chocolates than anybody else in the world. I'll bet I do. That makes me their number one customer."

"I don't doubt it," B said, grinning at her friend. She tossed a dart at the dartboard on the wall. It had the logo for Pluto Candies, her father's biggest competitor, taped right at the center of the bull's-eye. She missed. "Thanks for keeping my dad's job secure."

George looked out the window onto the large

factory room where workers packed cases of candy. "There goes a truckload of Caramelicious Cremes. And that lady? She's loading a pallet full of Mint Fizzes. That guy's got Peanut Butter Pillows." George slumped down in the office chair. "Oh, man. I'm in heaven."

"No, you're in my chair," B's dad said, entering at just that moment. "C'mon, George. If you think the pallet loading's good, you haven't seen anything yet. You, too, B. I've got a surprise for you both."

They followed Mr. Cicely down the corridor onto an elevator. George tugged on his sleeve. "Wanna hear my idea for what your next new chocolate should be? You'll love this."

"Actually, today . . ."

"It's a candy bar. You start with a simple, flat cracker base. A rectangle. Then you coat it with a layer of peanut brittle. See what I mean? A nice, crunchy, sweet layer of peanut brittle. Drizzle a little caramel over that, then dunk it in chocolate."

"Thanks George, I . . ." B could tell her dad had other things on his mind. But then he paused. "Wait. Did you say, peanut brittle over a cracker?"

George nodded.

"With caramel? Then chocolate?"

"That's right." George's chest was sticking out a mile.

The elevator doors opened, and they stepped out onto a shiny new wing of the factory that B had never seen before. Her dad was still mentally forming that new candy bar. His voice sounded far away. "The perfect combination of salty and sweet . . . crunchy and smooth . . . And nobody else has done it yet." He whipped out his Crystal Ballphone — any nonwitch would think it was a cell phone — and started punching buttons with his thumbs.

"What're you doing, Dad?" B asked.

"Just texting myself a note to have the kitchens try this out." He finished and snapped the phone shut, then ruffled George's hair. "Keep it under your hats, okay, guys? I may have to put you on the payroll, George."

B feared her friend might faint with happiness. "Better not," she said. "He'd eat sweets all day long. After a couple of weeks, you'd have to roll him out the door."

They came to a door, and B's dad swiped a

pass-card, which let them through. A second door, moments later, required a numeric code, and a third scanned his fingerprint.

"Where are you taking us, to meet the president?" George asked.

"Better than that," Mr. Cicely said. He lowered his voice to a whisper. "You will both get to see the dipping debut for our brand-new, top secret line of chocolates." He paused for impact. George's eyeballs looked ready to pop out of his head.

"What are they?" George begged.

"Enchanted Chocolates Fabulous Fruits!"

George's jaw dropped. "You mean, fruit dipped in chocolate?"

"Triple-dipped," Mr. Cicely said solemnly. "In our most deluxe, premium chocolate yet. First milk chocolate, then white chocolate, then dark."

George shook his head in wonder. "This is a day to remember for the rest of my *life*."

"Oh, toadspawn," B said. "I thought this was going to be something *good*. Fruit and chocolate together are gross. Blaugh."

George looked horrified. "Are you kidding? Chocolate-covered cherries?"

"Disgusting," B said. "They taste like cough medicine."

Mr. Cicely and George shared a pained look. They reached a security gate in the corridor, and B and George held out their arms while a guard scanned them using a strange beeping electrical device. "What's this for, Dad?" B asked.

"A search for contaminants," he explained. "There are those who would like to sabotage Enchanted Chocolates' new products. I know for a fact that Pluto Candies would pay any price for our secret recipes."

"Pluto Candies!" George scoffed. "They're not even in the same *universe*."

"You can say that again," B's dad said.

They reached a set of double doors. He pushed them open and ushered B and George inside.

"Holy cats! Look at this place!"

B gaped at the vast, modern production room, all decked out with stainless steel, glass, and tile, with funky, squiggly halogen lamps dangling from the ceiling. Spread across the production floor were large machines, draped in huge sheets of rainbow-colored cloth. A wide purple ribbon with a festive bow in the middle hung from wall to wall across the room.

"Come on over here and suit up," Mr. Cicely said. He led B and George to a corner where a large group of visitors stood, dressed in white suits, caps, gloves, and shoe covers.

"What's this about?" George asked.

"The chocolate cannot be compromised," Mr. Cicely said. "Stay here a minute, will you? I have a few last-minute things to take care of."

B and George helped each other put on their scratchy protective suits.

"You look like a spaceman, George," B said.

"Yeah? You look like a space alien."

B laughed aloud, then stopped.

"What's the matter?" George asked.

"It can't be," B whispered, staring at a white-suited form, partly obscured by a taller man. "It's bad enough having to put up with him at school. What would he be doing *here*?"

"Who? What?" George tried to get a better look.

B leaned closer to whisper in her best friend's ear. "It's Jason Jameson!"

Chapter 2

"Jason *Jameson*," George's whisper was a little too loud. "And they thought *we* might contaminate the chocolate? Who'd invite a stinker like him?"

"Ssh! He's coming this way!"

B's policy was to avoid her sixth-grade nemesis as much as possible. He never let slip an opportunity to annoy B or her friends. Whenever there was something shady, mean, or dishonest going on at school, chances were good that Jason Jameson was behind it.

Jason reached the spot where B and George were standing. "What are you two doing here?" he said. "They don't let just anyone show up to an Enchanted Chocolates launch."

"I agree," B said. "How did *you* get through security?"

Jason smiled smugly. "My dad's company supplied all the fruit for the new line of chocolates," he said. "Premiere Produce Incorporated. I'm sure you've heard of it."

"Nope," George said. "Can't say that I have."

Jason ignored him. "My dad consults with me on all his biggest accounts. He listens to my advice more than anyone else's."

"Oh, really?" B said, her blood boiling. "Well, my dad is the one in charge of the entire Enchanted Chocolates product line. He thought up Fabulous Fruits. And George and I have been consulting with my dad on an even more top secret line of chocolates," she added. "One that doesn't need any crummy fruit."

"Jason! C'mon over here a second. I want to introduce you to someone." The man in the white suit beckoning Jason had to be his father. They had the same plastering of freckles over their faces.

"Later, Fruitfly," Jason said. "Got to meet the VIP guests. Life of the party!" And laughing, he headed back to his dad.

"Ooh, he makes me so mad!" B muttered under

her breath. "Why does he have to be here today, and ruin the excitement?"

"Never mind him," George said. "But, er, how come you made up that stuff about us consulting on the new line of chocolates?"

"Well, it's sort of true, isn't it? I mean, you told Dad an idea just today, and he got excited about it." She sighed. "I *hate* how Jason acts like he's such a big deal, and everyone else is chopped liver."

"B, George," B's dad called. "Got some folks for you to meet. And someone you already know."

They hurried over to where he stood. B didn't at first glance recognize Mr. Bishop behind his white suit and hat. He was her English teacher and, secretly, her witching tutor. B didn't know the other gentleman, a thin bald man not yet in his protective gear, wearing an expensive-looking suit.

"Kids, meet Mayor Cumberland," B's dad said, indicating the man in the suit. "He's here to cut the ribbon for the launch ceremony. Mr. Bishop is my daughter's teacher, Mayor — did I ever mention that? He teaches school but does some advertising work for us on the side. We've asked him to write a song for the occasion. Want to hear it?"

They all nodded. B's dad drew Mayor Cumberland, B, and George a little distance away from the crowd. They gathered around Mr. Bishop to hear his song.

He coughed and smiled nervously, then sang in a pleasant but soft voice,

"Fabulous Fruits! Freshness with a triple dip.
Choco-fruity taste to make your taste buds flip!
Fruit has never been so exciting.
Chocolate layers, how inviting!
Enchanted Chocolates Fruit. That's Fabulicious!"

"Isn't it wonderful?" Mr. Cicely said, clapping Mr. Bishop on the back.

"Hmm, wonderful," the mayor told B's teacher, but he seemed impatient to get on with the ceremony.

"Oh, no," B whispered to George. "I am never going to get that song out of my head."

"It's fabulicious," George teased.

"Stop!" B groaned.

Mayor Cumberland finished getting his protective gear on and then B's father summoned everyone's attention again.

"Welcome, and thanks for joining us today for

the launch of Fabulous Fruits! And now it's time for our esteemed mayor, Wallace Cumberland, to make things official." He handed the mayor an enormous pair of scissors. "Ready to do the honors, Mayor?"

A newspaper photographer went down on one knee to snap a shot of the ribbon cutting. Mayor Cumberland got into position and took the scissors gingerly. He smiled confidently as the photographer aimed his huge camera at him.

"A few words to mark this occasion," he said, with the scissor blades paused over the ribbon. "On behalf of the citizens of this community, who count on Enchanted Chocolates to make all our lives so much . . . sweeter" — he paused for people to laugh — "this new concoction is almost ready to take on the world!" And he snipped the ribbon.

Everyone applauded. B's dad smiled and said, "I have to respectfully disagree, Mayor. Here at Enchanted Chocolates, we think it is *completely* ready to take on the world!"

Everyone laughed. Then he nodded to the workers stationed by each of the machines. They pulled off the brightly colored drapes with a dramatic swish. Then, together, B's dad and Mr. Jameson each flipped a large switch. All around the room, machines hummed to life. Workers tumbled tubs of strawberries, apricots, cherries, blueberries, pine-apple pieces, and peach slices into hoppers that routed fruit on conveyor belts. Large-paddled stir-rers began mixing vats of creamy chocolate, sending waves of heavenly chocolate vapor wafting into the air.

Along with all the other visitors, B and George pressed closer, eager for a glimpse of the first can-dies to come out. No one spoke. Everyone seemed paused, poised on tiptoe for the unveiling of the first Fabulous Fruit.

There was a loud bang.

Like popping corn, one by one, the lights went out. The room was plunged into total darkness.

Chapter 3

Silence, for only a second. Then a woman screamed.

People seemed to be moving about. B heard scuffling feet and people crying out that others had stepped on their toes. Murmurs rose to an anxious pitch before B's dad's voice broke through.

"Ladies and gentlemen, will everyone please stay calm and remain where you are while we fix the lights? We don't want anyone bumping into machinery and getting hurt. Thank you." He paused. "We should have the lights back on in no time."

B felt George lean closer to her, and reach for her arm. "That you, B?"

"Yep, George, it's me."

He lowered his voice to a small whisper. "Did you have anything to do with this?"

B's pulse quickened. She couldn't have caused this, could she? Her magic had a way of going haywire. "I don't see how I could have, George," she whispered back. "I didn't say or spell a thing. Not a single thing." She shook her head, forgetting that in the dark George couldn't see. "I didn't do this. But I think I can help fix it." She concentrated on the lamps overhead. What had they looked like? Oh, yes. She could imagine them now. "L-I-G-H-T," she whispered.

More popping sounds, as one by one the lights around the factory blinked then glowed.

B looked around the relieved crowd of visitors. Her father stood next to Jason's dad, still near the switches on the wall. Mr. Bishop and Mayor Cumberland stood near one of the chocolate vats, and Jason Jameson — of course! — stood near the conveyor belt where, any second, the first Fabulous Fruits were about to pop out.

All over the room, the fleet of candy-making machines still chugged and dipped. Fabulous Fruits piled up at the end of the conveyor belts, their still-wet chocolate coatings glistening. Even though she knew there was fruit inside, B had to admit they looked delicious. Jason clearly thought so, too. Wait! Was he *chewing*?

She marched over to where he stood, ready to confront him for having eaten candy right off the conveyor belt. That was strictly against the rules, she knew, from many previous visits with her dad. And if she didn't nab him soon, he'd stuff his face with the avalanche of chocolate-coated fruit that was now pouring out on the conveyor belts, almost faster than the workers could tote it off in large bins to prepare for packaging.

"Jason Jame — *whoa!*" B's sneaker slipped in something, and she fell, *kersplat*, face-first on the factory floor. Her knees and her hands stung where she'd caught herself, but otherwise she wasn't hurt. Mr. Bishop and Mayor Cumberland, who stood nearest, hurried over, asking B repeatedly if she was all right. Each of them went to help her up, bonking heads with each other in the process. At last, assisted by both her rescuers, B was back on her feet, just in time to see Jason, his open mouth stuffed with chocolate fruit, laughing at her.

Ohhh, that Jason . . . B almost stomped her foot, but she remembered the slippery stuff on the floor and looked down. A shimmery blue puddle swirled around her white-covered sneakers. She bent for a closer look. Cleaning solution? No, B felt pretty sure it wasn't. It almost looked like a potion. But before she could touch it, Mr. Bishop wiped up the spill with his handkerchief. His eyes met B's, but she couldn't quite read what they were saying.

"We're back in business, folks," B's dad said. "Never a dull moment in the chocolate factory." He waved at an employee, who carried a platter with fresh samples over to the group. "I want to thank you all for being here today to celebrate the launch of this terrific new product. As you can imagine, we're pretty excited about Fabulous Fruits here at Enchanted Chocolates. We want you to be the first to taste them. Please, step on up and try a sample."

George appeared at B's side. "Oh, man, I can't wait," he said. "To think, I get to be one of the first!" He gave B a nudge with his elbow. "Hey, B, are you auditioning to become the next Enchanted Chocolates candy yourself?"

B shook her head. "You know, George, you're losing your grip. For a joke, that one just didn't make sense. No punch line at all."

"It's no joke. You're covered in chocolate!"

B craned her neck around and lifted her arm to see that there were chocolate handprints all over her back. "How did that happen?" She snapped her fingers. "I know. Mr. Bishop and Mayor Cumberland helped me up when I tripped. One of them must have touched some chocolate by mistake when the lights went out."

Jason cut to the head of the line of people eager to sample their first-ever Fabulous Fruits. And he'd already had some! Mr. Cicely picked up a candy with a pair of silver tongs and was just about to drop it into Jason's outstretched hand, when Mr. Jameson pulled Jason aside.

"Time we were leaving, son," he said.

"Awww, Dad," Jason whined. "I just wanted to try *one* of the Fabulous Fruits. One little one."

"Don't try to kid me," Jason's dad said in a much lower, sterner voice. "It's too late for you to try 'just one.' Wipe that chocolate off your mouth."

Around the room, guests turned toward the

source of the argument. They stared at Jason and his dad.

Mr. Jameson gave an unconvincing laugh. "Please excuse us both, we must be going now," he said, leading Jason toward the door. "Jason's tired after a long day at school. Hard work maintaining those honor roll grades, isn't it, son?"

B glanced at George. *Oh, brother.* Like father, like son.

"But, Dad, everyone else gets to have chocolate." Jason's voice was much lower now, but B and George still heard him.

"Let them destroy their health, then," his father replied. "Fruit is nature's candy. You know better than to raise a fuss like this." They left.

George and B reached the head of the line. When her father held out a Fabulous Fruit for her to try, B shook her head, but George popped a chocolate-covered apricot into his mouth and chewed slowly. B's dad watched his face. He took a chocolate-covered cherry for himself and put it in his mouth.

"Well, George? What do you say?"

George seemed to be concentrating on chewing. He gulped down his candy.

"It's, uh, it sure is fruity."

"But is it fabulous?" B's dad pressed him.

George nodded once. "Uh, yeah. Fabulous. Yeah, it's good. Really." He gave B's dad a thumbs-up sign. Mr. Cicely, visibly delighted, moved on with his platter.

When he was out of earshot, George pulled B aside and whispered, "B, it's *awful!*"

"Well, that's no surprise. I told you chocolate and fruit don't mix!"

George shook his head. "It's not that. I like chocolate and fruit. Something's wrong with this chocolate."

"But you love Enchanted Chocolate. It's the same stuff as all their other candies. Better, Dad said."

"This tastes . . . strange. Bitter. Can chocolate go rotten?"

B shrugged. "I guess so. But this is fresh, new chocolate." She watched her friend closely. "George, if it tastes so bad, how come you told Dad you liked it?"

George sighed. "Look at him. He's so excited, with all these people here. Would you want to be the one to tell him that his big new product stinks?"

Chapter 4

" 'Fabulous Fruits, freshness with a triple dip,' "
Mr. Cicely sang that evening as he drove B and
George home after the last guests had left. "Catchy
tune, eh? *Enchanted Chocolates Fruit. That's
Fabulicious!*' "

Oh, great. Now the tune was going to be stuck
in B's head again.

"Today was a great day. Even though we had
the problem with the lights. A really successful product launch. A week from now, we've got ads appearing
in magazines and websites all over the country." He
snapped his fingers. "Do you think your friend in the
rock band might sing the jingle for us in a TV ad?"

"Um, maybe," B said, thinking of her friend
Trina, the famous singer in the Black Cats, who just
happened to be a sixth-grader in B's class. Sure,

Trina might agree to sing, but if this chocolate tasted as bad as George said, was that a good idea?

"*Ah-ah-choo!*" B's dad sneezed and shook his head. "Phew! That was a big one. Off the Richter scale, eh?"

B blinked. She could have sworn she saw a trio of blue bubbles appear, then pop, right when her father sneezed. It must have been a trick of light from the setting sun coming through the windshield.

"We're going to need to hire you at Enchanted Chocolates, George," B's dad said. "Chief Taster and Idea Generator."

"Awesome!" George said, bouncing in his seat. "I could drop out of school and eat chocolate all day long!"

"Whoa! Hold on, there. You'll need to finish school to work for me. *Ah-choo!*"

No doubt about it. Dozens of blue bubbles appeared in the front seat. Her father waved them away quickly.

"You must be catching cold," George said.

"Nope. He's probably allergic to chocolate-covered fruit," said B. "I know I am."

"Ha-ha. Very funny." B's dad pulled into their driveway, and they all climbed out of the car and went inside.

B's mom was just pulling a steaming pan of manicotti out of the oven, stuffed with a special filling of goat cheese, minced thistles, roasted nettles, and wild mushrooms. She set it down next to a basket of freshly buttered garlic bread and a large wooden bowl of tossed salad. Mrs. Cicely was a championship finalist in the Witchin' Kitchen competitions, and almost every meal at their home was a culinary adventure — although whenever nonwitch guests like George were around, she downplayed her witchy ingredients.

"Hi, guys, how was the launch?" Mrs. Cicely asked them. "Stay for dinner, George?"

Quick as a flash, George slipped into a chair and tucked his napkin into his collar. "Yes, please. That pasta dish smells incredible. What's in it?"

"Oh, cheese. And stuff," Mrs. Cicely said, pouring pomegranate vinaigrette over the salad.

"Fabulous Fruits for dessert," B's dad said, setting a box of the new candy on the kitchen counter. He sniffed loudly and rubbed his nose.

B's mom got out a set of drippy red candles stuck into old green bottles and lit the candles. "For atmosphere," she said. "Imagine we're in Italy. Why don't you fetch that box of tissues from upstairs, Felix?"

"Good idea," said B's dad. "I think I — *ah-choo!*"

The candles blew themselves out. B and her mom exchanged glances, and Mrs. Cicely's eyebrows rose.

Mr. Cicely was already halfway up the stairs and unaware. *"Ah-choo! Ah-choo!"*

Two glasses of ice water tipped simultaneously. B and her mom both jumped up to grab towels. *That's weird*, thought B as she mopped up the liquid.

"Aaaaaah-aaah-CHOO!" they heard from upstairs.

Salad ingredients rose up from their wooden bowl and started re-tossing themselves in the air, while the cruet of red dressing flung splashes of vinaigrette in every direction and croutons crunched in midair.

Holy cats! What on earth was going on?

"B, dear, don't you and George have, er, things to do before dinner?" B's mom said loudly, jumping in between George and the table and shooting B a panicked look. George wasn't supposed to know about magic. B had never told her parents that she'd accidentally let the secret slip to her best friend. But right now, she needed to play along — and hoped George would, too.

"Hey, George," B said. "Come see that, er, magazine I was telling you about. It's in the living room."

B barely heard her mother's urgent whisper, *"Candles light, evaporate spill; lettuce, tomatoes, and cukes, be still!"*

George blinked. "What magazine? I don't remember you mentioning a magazine."

"You know," B said, "the *magazine*?"

"Oh, right," George said, catching on at last. "*That* magazine." And he rose to follow B out of the room.

"Sorry, guys," B's mom said. "You'll have to look at your magazine later on. Right now it's time for George to get home. You don't want to miss your dinner, do you?"

George's face fell. "But . . . pasta . . . cheese . . . didn't you just ask me to eat dinner here?"

B's mom turned toward the counter and pretended to wipe a spill. "Did I? Oh, I'm sorry, George, how thoughtless of me. I'm afraid there isn't enough to go around."

George stared at the gigantic pan of manicotti wafting its saucy scent over the kitchen.

"Dawn's sure to be hungry when she gets home later. And you know B and her appetite," Mrs. Cicely continued, still avoiding looking at George. "I saw your mother out in your yard today, and she mentioned that she was making stuffed cabbage leaves tonight. You won't want to miss that!"

"Stuffed cabbage leaves!" George was in agony. He looked to B for help, but she grabbed him by the elbow and steered him toward the door.

"C'mon," she said. "If I can suppress my monster appetite, maybe I can save you some. Walk you home?"

"Aaah-CHOOO!"

The sink faucets began turning on and off.

"And anyway," B's mom added apologetically,

"you wouldn't want to catch this cold that it appears B's father has got."

Once they were outside, B patted her friend's shoulder. "Sorry about that, George. Something odd's going on with Dad's magic, and Mom was just worried about you finding out. This kind of thing has never happened before."

George stopped in his tracks and looked at B. "You mean, that wasn't you making all those crazy things happen?"

B laughed out loud. "Of course not. Why would I?"

George shrugged. "I don't know, but if it wasn't you, then what's going on?"

B remembered the panicked look on her mother's face. "I wish I knew."

Chapter 5

"B, what's gotten into you?" B's mother asked when she returned to their kitchen. "You can't be careless like that with your magic when others are around!"

B shook her head. "It wasn't me, Mom, I swear. I wasn't spelling a thing." To herself, she thought, *Why does everyone blame me when magic gets messy?*

"Hmmm."

B felt hurt that her mother would suspect her of being so careless. It wasn't like her mom to jump to conclusions like that. Just then, her dad slumped into a chair at the kitchen table, a box of tissues in one hand.

"Ugh," he said, his voice sounding thick and congested. "Don't know where this cold came from. *Aah-choo!*"

The freezer door flew open, and a container of pistachio gelato from the Magical Moo Creamery flew out and landed in his lap.

B's mom looked at her husband as though she was seeing him for the first time. *"Felix?"*

He looked as groggy as a bear coming out of hibernation. "Hm? What? *Aah-choo!"*

The refrigerator door opened and out flew the bottle of Enchanted Chocolate Sundae Sauce, landing right next to the gelato.

"It's you!" B's mom said. "Your *sneezing.* That's what's causing this. But why?"

"I don't know," B's dad said in a stuffy voice. "I guess it must be a witch cold."

"I thought we were immunized against those," B said.

"I thought so, too," her mother said. "You need to see a doctor. And B? I'm sorry I blamed you."

B smiled, feeling relieved. "That's okay."

"There's no need to bother the doctor over a minor sniffle," insisted Mr. Cicely. *"Aah-ah-aaah-chooooooo!"*

They braced themselves, searching the room for the results of the sneeze. Then B saw her father's face and gasped. Big, angry-looking purple warts were popping out, one by one, all over his face and hands!

He groped at his cheeks and winced whenever he touched a wart. Then he held out his hands and gazed at them in horror.

"Felix!" B's mother cried. "That's it. You're seeing the doctor this instant!" She whipped out her Crystal Ballphone and dialed the witch doctor, Dr. Jellicoe. Within minutes a little tornado of wind swept into the kitchen, and when it stopped, there stood the short, round, jovial form of Marcellus K. Jellicoe, Doctor of Magical Medicine.

Dr. Jellicoe beamed and waved a big pink lollipop in the air. B knew, from the time she'd gone to see him herself, that he believed most any magical malady could be treated with a watermelon lollipop. But when the doctor saw her father's purple warts, he gulped, and slipped the candy back into his lab coat pocket. "Well, well," he said. "What have we here?"

B's mom explained about the random magical mishaps that happened whenever her husband sneezed, and Dr. Jellicoe nodded gravely. He turned to his patient. "Let's just see where we are, then, shall we? Why don't you go ahead and perform a nice simple spell. Easy-peasy. See if you can fill that empty glass with, oh, I don't know, a chocolate milkshake."

B's dad blew his nose, then tried:

"Fill the glass, don't let it break.

Please pour me a ch . . . chicken sandwich."

B giggled. Her dad could sure be a joker! But her mom shook her head, and Dr. Jellicoe pressed his lips together.

"Try again, shall we?" the doctor said. "You've got food on the mind, it seems. Are you hungry? Do any food spell you want. Load your plate up with dinner. Go on, give it a try."

"Hot manicotti, if you please.

I like mine with Parmesan pudding."

He pressed his fingers into his temples. "Parmesan *pudding*? What's the matter with me, Doc? Is it serious?"

"I'm afraid it is," Dr. Jellicoe said. "To lose one's rhyming ability . . . well, that's just not something we like to see." He tapped his chin. "I'd like to consult with a colleague on this case. He's a specialist, the head of health at the Magical Rhyming Society. Do you mind, Madame?"

B's mother shook her head and offered Dr. Jellicoe the use of her Crystal Ballphone. In minutes another traveling spell blew into the kitchen, and B was surprised to see Mayor Wallace Cumberland standing there in his slick black suit, leather gloves, and a shiny leather briefcase in one hand.

"You're the head of health?" B said.

Mayor Cumberland looked down at B. "I am," he said with a sniff.

"But you're the mayor. Which is your real job?"

B's mom placed a hand on her shoulder. "Many witches have jobs in both the outside world and the witching community, B," she said. She added a little squeeze, which B understood to mean, "Be polite!"

"We've got a bad case, here, Wally," Dr. Jellicoe said. "This gentlewitch has lost his rhyming ability completely. Can't form a spell to save his supper. First accidents, then warts, and now Spellulus Interruptus. What do you suggest?"

Mayor Cumberland looked B's father up and down. He pulled a pair of glasses from his inner jacket pocket and polished the lenses on his sleeve. Finally he reached into his briefcase, pulled out a magnifying glass, and held it up in front of B's dad's eyeball. When B's dad blinked, the head of health straightened up. He lifted a section of his patient's hair and frowned at his scalp. Then he poked his finger into B's dad's tummy.

"Mayor Cumberland, what could it be?" B's mom said. "You're our health specialist. Surely you've come across such cases before?"

Mayor Cumberland frowned and slipped his glasses back into his pocket. "Looks to me like his Vitamin R supply is dangerously deficient — a common side effect of eating too many sweets and chocolate."

"Vitamin R?" B repeated. "Never heard of that."

"Short for 'Vitamin Rhyme,'" the mayor said. "Only thing for it, in cases like this, is to chew on pages of a rhyming dictionary. That will boost the R reserves. And stay away from the sweet stuff, of course."

B's mom took a long look at Mayor Cumberland. "Did you just say *eat pages*?" She shook her head.

"Well, you *are* the specialist. B, run to the bookshelf and bring back that old rhyming dictionary that we hardly ever use anymore."

B returned with the book and tore out a few sheets, which she handed to her father.

The scowl on his face spoke volumes. "You want me to eat that?"

"A glass of water will help," Mayor Cumberland said. "Have a bite."

Looking like he'd rather be getting a cavity drilled without anesthesia, B's dad took a tentative nibble from the dictionary pages.

"More," the mayor instructed. B's dad took another bite.

"Look!" B said. "The spots. They're fading."

Her father took bigger bites, and one by one the purple warts receded and vanished.

"See?" Mayor Cumberland said. "What did I tell you?"

"I knew you could solve the mystery," Dr. Jellicoe said, clapping the mayor on the back, which took the head of health by surprise.

"Try a spell, Felix," B's mom said.

B's dad tried a rhyme:

"This malady has made me droop.
I'd love a bowl of chicken stroganoff."

He shook his head. "No good."

B could see the worry written all over his face. His tongue was stained black from the ink, and he looked miserable. B's mom placed a comforting hand on his arm.

B thought for a moment that Mayor Cumberland looked worried, too, but then Dr. Jellicoe stepped in. "Give it time; give it time," Dr. Jellicoe said. "Get plenty of rest, and drown that cold with dictionary pages and fluids. You'll get your magic back in no time."

"Are you sure?" B's dad said, eyeing a page of rhyming "D" words with disgust.

"As sure as Enchanted Chocolates makes scrumptious chocolates time after time!" Mayor Cumberland said with full confidence.

B bit her lip. According to George, that wasn't as sure as it once was, either.

Chapter 6

The next morning, as B hurried from homeroom to art class, she pulled a shiny box out of her backpack to show the other kids before the teacher, Miss Willow, arrived. Her father had given her Fabulous Fruits to share with her friends. It was part of his strategy to spread the word about the new candy.

"Chocolate, anyone?"

In seconds she was mobbed. Everyone jostled for their chance to snag the candy of their choice — everyone, that is, except Jason Jameson, who stood at a distance, a frown plastered on his freckled face. *He wants one,* B thought, *but he's too stuck-up to take anything I'm sharing.*

B's good friend Trina walked in and dropped her plaid backpack on her seat. Her full name was Katrina Lang, an everyday sixth-grader who also happened to be "Kat," the lead singer of the Black Cats, a superstar pop group at the top of the charts. When she first moved to B's town she tried to keep that fact a secret, but it wasn't long before B and George found out. Now everyone knew, and they'd mostly stopped spazzing out about it. Her real secret, which no other kids but B and George knew, was that Trina was also a witch.

"Whatcha got, B?" Trina said, coming over to investigate the commotion.

"New chocolates my dad gave me to share," B said. "You would have gotten some yesterday, if you hadn't had Black Cats practice."

"Sorry," Trina said, grinning. "What are they?"

"Fabulous Fruits, dipped in three kinds of chocolate. Want some?"

Trina peered into the box. The first layer was nearly finished and the crumpled wrappers lay scattered. She shook her head. "No thanks. Not just yet. Too early in the morning for candy."

Later, in English class, B sat in her usual seat next to George and near Trina. She left the chocolates on her desk and went over to greet Mozart, the classroom pet hamster, and refill his water dish. She returned to her desk just as Mr. Bishop arrived and began announcing the day's assignment. It looked like several chocolates were missing. No matter — everyone was welcome to them. But when Mr. Bishop started writing on the blackboard, George slipped her a note.

Jason swiped a handful of chocolates, the note read. *He was acting all sneaky about it, like he was stealing them.*

B looked around to make sure Mr. Bishop didn't see her passing notes, then took out her pencil and wrote, *That's weird. I would have given him some. Dad wanted me to share with everyone. Did you try any today?*

George read the note and shook his head no. There were only a couple left in the box, so B put them away for George.

When the bell rang at the end of English class, and Mr. Bishop and most of the other students had filed out of the room, B reopened the box to give George the last few candies. She was hoping the taste would be back to normal now.

"How are they, George?" B said. "Any better than yesterday?"

George nibbled thoughtfully, swallowed, and shook his head. "Nope. Same," he said. "B, I really should talk to your dad. I think maybe he's so excited about this launch that his taste buds aren't working like they ought to. Can we stop at Enchanted Chocolates after school?"

"That would be amazing!" Trina said. "I've always wanted to see inside a chocolate factory."

B packed her backpack and stood. "I don't know. Dad's sick, but he still went to work today because a bunch of his employees called in sick this morning. He's probably super busy, and super tired."

"I won't take much of his time," George said. "Can't we just stop by his office for a few minutes?"

B hesitated. "Oh, all right. Just for a few minutes. I'd kind of like to check on him and see how he's feeling anyway. C'mon, let's go eat."

They each stopped at their lockers. B was just about to head to the caf when a tall girl with a scarf over her head and neck grabbed her hand.

"Hey!" B said. She turned to peer under the girl's scarf. "Dawn? Is that you?"

The hooded figure nodded. "Help me, B," she

said, her voice weak and scratchy. "Look!" She lifted the scarf, and B gasped to see thick purple spots bubbling out all over her sister's usually flawless complexion.

"Jumping jinxes, Dawn, are you okay?"

Dawn shook her head. "I'm exhausted. I've got to get home to bed, before anyone sees me. I was worried you were sick, too, but you look fine." She blew her nose loudly. "All morning, every time I sneezed, my teachers got a new fashion accessory, poof!" She blew her nose again. "The styles got lamer and lamer. It was awful!"

"C'mon, let me take you to the office. I'll call Mom and tell her to come pick you up."

"Then that stopped," Dawn said, as though she hadn't heard B, "but these nasty boils appeared. What if my face is scarred for life? How will I get my senior portrait taken?"

B led Dawn by the arm down the long corridor to the main office. "That's years away," B said. "You've got the same symptoms Dad had last night. The spots went away when he chewed on pages from the rhyming dictionary. But it didn't help his magic any."

"Ugh, gross," Dawn moaned. "I don't want to eat ink." She sneezed, and a nearby locker flew open. "I got text messages on my Crystal Ballphone from Stef and Macey. They both went home sick today, too. Same purple spots. What's weird is, I just saw them last night at a witching class party, and they seemed fine."

"So did you, though, right?" B said.

"Yeah, I guess so," Dawn agreed.

"What'd you do at the party?"

"Not much. Just told each other's fortunes — *aaaaah-chooo!* — and then ate pizza and some of Dad's new Fabulous Fruits."

"Doesn't sound dangerous," B said.

Dawn held up her hand and showed B a new purple welt that had just appeared there. "I'm hideous! Am I going to lose my magic, too?"

"Try a rhyme," B urged. "Anything. Some simple thing that no one would notice." She reached into her schoolbag and pulled out a stubby pencil. "Try sharpening my pencil magically."

Dawn's bleary red eyes blinked as she tried to focus on the pencil.

"Let's hope my magic won't disappoint.

Grind B's pencil to a nice, sharp pants."

She shook herself. *"Pants?* A nice, sharp . . . pajamas! No. Pumps? What's the matter with me?"

"Ssssh," B cautioned as her sister's anxious voice rose. "Never mind. Dad had the same thing. You just need to rest."

"I don't know," Dawn said, wiping her nose with a tissue. "I just hope the Board of Magical Health comes up with a cure or something soon."

B steered her sister into the office. "I'm sure they will. You'll feel better in no time. Sit here and relax, while I call Mom."

B smiled to reassure her sister, but her mind was spinning. *Why are so many witches getting sick all of a sudden? Why are they losing their magic?*

And will I be next?

Chapter 7

That afternoon, when B, George, and Trina reached Enchanted Chocolates, the receptionist, Janika, greeted them with a smile, then paged B's dad to let him know they were there. B's dad told Janika to issue the kids security badges so they could come join him in the Fabulous Fruits wing. They headed down the halls.

The security checkpoints they'd passed through the day before were empty. When they reached the fruit-dipping machines and had put on their white safety suits, B's dad greeted them with a halfhearted smile. B was glad to see that her father's purple spots were completely gone, and he didn't appear to be sneezing anymore. But he sure didn't look like his usual cheerful self. His hair stood straight up, like it always did when he was worried, because he'd run his hands through his hair so many times.

"How're you doing, Dad?" B asked.

"Not so great," her father answered. "So many workers are out sick that we can't run all the dipping machines, and we've got a lot of sample-size packages of Fabulous Fruits to fill and send to candy stores around the country. We're way behind schedule."

"No, I meant, how are you *feeling*?" B asked. "You know? Your, er, *cold*?"

"Ah." He nodded. "Somewhat better, but not one hundred percent."

"Dawn seems to be *catching cold*, too," B said. "She went home early from school today, *sneezing* a lot."

B's dad frowned. B knew he understood what she was really telling him. His forehead creased with worry. "Poor Dawn."

George tugged on his sleeve. "Um, can I talk to you about the chocolate? From yesterday? You know, some feedback?"

B's dad ran his fingers through his hair again. "Sure, George. What's on your mind?"

George looked like he was working hard not to hurt B's dad's feelings. "You know I'm Enchanted Chocolates' number one fan, right? So, I know how good your chocolate always is." He swallowed. "The chocolate in Enchanted Fruits isn't good. It's just not as delicious as your chocolates normally are."

B's dad listened intently to George. Even after George finished speaking, he stood there rubbing his scalp for a moment. Then he snapped his fingers. "You only tried it yesterday, correct?"

"And today, too," George said. "The ones that B brought to school."

B's dad nodded. "That would do it. Makes sense — the machines were brand-new. It could be that the machines weren't mixing the chocolate ingredients together properly. The proportions may have been wrong. I'm sure it will taste better to you now. Let's have you try a fresh batch."

He poured a big bowl of strawberries into the hopper of a nearby dipping machine, then flipped the switch. A wheel of mechanical arms began to spin, then the claw at the end of each arm plucked up a fat red berry and dipped it in all three chocolate flavors. A jet of frigid air gave a quick flash-freeze to each chocolate coating to help it set faster. In no time, shiny Fabulous Fruit strawberries were rolling out on the conveyor belt.

"Trina? George? Help yourself, and please, tell me what you *really* think of them."

Trina sank her teeth into her Fabulous Fruit, and closed her eyes. "Mmmm! That's scrumptious!"

B's dad rubbed his palms together and grinned. "I knew it! I knew the machines just needed to get warmed up to mix the chocolate right."

George chewed his chocolate and slowly shook his head. "I hate to disappoint you, but the chocolate's still not right."

"Why not, George?" Trina said, popping another berry in her mouth. "I think it tastes great!"

"Well, sure," George said. "Enchanted Chocolate makes the best chocolate in the world. Even on a bad day. Mediocre Enchanted Chocolate is still better than anything else. And this chocolate" — he pointed to the half-eaten berry in his hand — "is just that. Mediocre. There's a funny aftertaste. Some people might not notice it, but I" — he made a little bow — "I am a chocolate expert."

"Aaah-chooo!"

A dipping machine worker, just passing by, let out an enormous sneeze, and the rotating wheel of fruit-dipping arms began spinning at triple speed, shooting berries all over the floor.

"Uh-oh," B's dad said with an uneasy glance at George, "machine malfunction! B, why don't you and your friends go up to my office and play darts till I get this cleaned up, okay?"

"Aaah-chooo!"

Another worker produced an earsplitting sneeze, and a tub of fresh pineapple slices transformed into miniature palm trees.

"Bert! Miranda! Looks like you're not feeling well," B's dad said in a loud voice. "Let me take you down to the infirmary so you can rest." He steered them both out the door. *Poor Dad*, B thought.

The Fabulous Fruit room was empty now except for B and her friends. The machines lay still, the vats of chocolates sat unstirred.

"Weren't you saying earlier, B, that a bunch of workers were out sick today?" George asked. "There must be some kind of epidemic going around here."

"No kidding," B said, looking sadly at the empty room. "Seems like all the Enchanted Chocolates workers are catching it."

"I wonder why," Trina said.

"Hey, Trina," said George, "how do you make an apple turnover?"

Trina stared at him like he had bats flying out of his ears. "I don't know. How?"

"You roll it down hill!" George hooted with laughter.

Trina rolled her eyes.

"What do you call a grouchy fruit?" George said.

"What?" Trina said reluctantly.

"A *crab* apple!"

B was used to George's jokes, so she paid him no attention. An idea had begun to form in her mind. "Jumping jinxes," she said. "I think I'm onto something."

"What?" George and Trina said at the same time.

B paced slowly around the room, thinking aloud as she did. "Enchanted Chocolate workers," she said. "Dad. Dawn. Dawn's friends. What do they all have in common?"

George and Trina looked at each other. "We don't know," Trina said. "What *do* they have in common? What's going on with Dawn and her friends?"

"They're sick, too," B said. "And you know why I think they are?"

"Why?" George and Trina asked at the same time.

"They all ate Fabulous Fruits!"

Trina dropped the chocolate-covered strawberry she'd just bitten into the trash, then scrubbed her hands on her jeans furiously, as if to wipe away the contaminated candy. George put a hand over his mouth.

"Dad ate some," B said, numbering people on her fingers. "All the workers got a taste. Dawn ate some. Her friends did — Dad gave her a box to take to her get-together. The only reason I'm still healthy," B went on, still pacing, "is because I never ate any Fabulous Fruits."

Trina looked positively green.

"Wait a minute," George said. "I'm still healthy." He cleared his throat and sniffed. "I mean, I *think* I am. Do I look sick to you?"

B studied his face. Same old George, his blue

eyes half hidden by his glasses and his mop of curly yellow hair. "Nope," she said. "You look healthy as a lizard."

"So what's the difference?" Trina said. "How come everyone is sick except George?"

B circled around George, thinking, thinking. Then it hit her. It was so obvious! How could she have missed it?

"Because you're not a witch, George," she said. "Everyone who works here . . . Dawn and all her witchy friends . . . They're sick. But you're not. Of course! Why didn't we see it? The symptoms of the illness are obviously magical — bogus spells spouting all over the place. It's got to be a witch-only sickness."

The relief on George's face was immense. B turned to Trina. "I'm sorry, Trina," she said, "but I think you're going to get sick."

Trina tried to shrug it off but B could tell Trina was worried.

"I don't understand it," said George. "This factory's as clean as an operating room. They've got all that security to make sure the chocolate's not contaminated. How could it be making people sick?"

"You've got to tell your dad, B," Trina said. "He's got to stop making the chocolate. He shouldn't give away any more samples, either."

B's ear caught the sound of footsteps approaching down the hall. "That's Dad, coming back," she said. "You guys wait here, while I go talk to him."

B intercepted her father in the hallway and told him what she'd figured out. "Something in the chocolate — I mean, something in Fabulous Fruits — is making witches sick, Dad," she said. "Every witch who's tried them is now ill. You've got to stop making them."

B's dad raked his hair with his hands once again. "Oh, dear," he said, realizing that B was right. "I'm afraid you're right, B. All that beautiful chocolate, wasted. Truckloads of premium fruit! And no explanation I can think of that makes any sense."

B squeezed her father's hand. "I know. It's a mystery."

"One thing is certain," he said. "We've got to get to the bottom of this. The Magical Rhyming Society needs to be told so they can treat all the sick witches. And they'll need to come here to help us figure out what magical sickness this is actually spreading."

"You'd better go tell them right away," B said. But her father shook his head.

"My magic still doesn't work," he said. "I'll need you to take the message for me. Have you learned how to transport yet?"

B gulped. Sort of, yes. But this was a big deal, her father letting her travel alone and entrusting her with an important message like this. She didn't want to seem lacking in confidence.

"Yep," she said truthfully. "I have learned how."

"Then, there's no time to lose," her father said. "I'll go in there and distract George and Trina while you transport. Hurry!"

Chapter 8

The door swung behind B's dad as he reentered the Fabulous Fruits room. B knew she only had a few minutes to transport to the M.R.S., notify Madame Mel, Grande Mistress of the Magical Rhyming Society, and get back again before her dad started getting nervous that George and Trina would notice she was missing.

Okay. Transportation spell. She had done it before, during magic tutoring sessions with Mr. Bishop, but there'd been a few mishaps. Focus. That was the key. You had to really focus on where you were going.

She tried to clear her mind and imagine herself in the M.R.S. She pictured the towering bookshelves in the main library, filled with sparkling volumes of magical books, guarded by floating librarian apparitions. She pictured the tall towers where once her traveling spell had landed her — whoops! Better not think about that. . . . B refocused her thoughts on the inside, where Madame Mel could always be found, striding around the corridors, her powder blue hair in a bun, her purple spectacles perched on the tip of her long nose, and her multicolored robe tinkling with thousands of silver magical charms.

"T-R-A-V-E-L," she said, then looked both ways to make sure no one in the corridor felt the rushing cyclonic wind that signaled a traveling spell. It whipped B's hair into her eyes and made the fabric of her shirt flap. But sure enough, it deposited her at the M.R.S. — unfortunately, on a pile of parchment that Madame Mel herself was trying to write on, atop a table in the library.

"Good afternoon, Beatrix," Madame Mellifluous said, without even looking up.

"How did you know it was me?" B asked, fearing and expecting to hear the Grande Mistress comment on B's notorious magical near misses.

"I recognized your sneakers. What can I do for you?"

B jumped down from the table and explained everything to Madame Mel about Fabulous Fruits and the epidemic of magical mumps, or whatever they were, spreading to every witch who tried the chocolate.

Madame Mel polished her spectacles on her sleeve, frowning. "I overheard something about a magical malady this morning, in the elevator," she said. "We'll need to look into it immediately." She snapped her fingers, and her magical robes transformed instantly into an official-looking lab coat and trousers. Her blue hair became gray, and the scroll of parchment she'd been holding became a clipboard. Only her purple glasses gave a hint of Madame Mel's usual fashion style.

The Grande Mistress of the M.R.S. took B's hand and said,

"To Enchanted Chocolates, in a magical flurry.
And tell my emergency team to hurry!"

Another traveling wind whipped up, but Madame Mel's spell was so skilled, it didn't even stir the papers on the library table. In seconds they stood in the hallway outside the Fabulous Fruits room, right where B had started.

"The dipping machines are in here," B began.

Whoosh! Whoosh! Whoosh!

More witches swept into the corridor on travel tornados of their own, each of them dressed in lab coats like Madame Mel's. Six got into place behind Madame Mel and together they marched into the dipping room, their clipboards at the ready. B ran to follow.

Her dad was giving George and Trina a demonstration of how the white chocolate mixer worked. His eyebrows rose at the sight of Madame Mel and her posse of witches in lab coats.

"Health inspectors," Madame Mel said abruptly. "Here to examine the sanitation of your facility."

"Er . . . of course," Mr. Cicely said. He gave B a secret wink. She knew it meant, "Thanks."

The magical "health inspectors" spread around the room, peering through magnifying glasses and using syringes and tongs to place samples of fruit and chocolate in test tubes. One inspector turned on a dipping machine, but the stirring paddles weren't properly lowered, and his white lab jacket was spattered with chocolate.

Madame Mel approached the largest dipping

machine and examined the vats

milk, white, and dark. She whipped a s

out of the pocket of her lab coat and began

a sample of chocolate from each vat. When

reached the milk chocolate, she pursed her lips.

"This chocolate doesn't taste right," she said.

"I know!" George cried. "That's what I've been saying."

Madame Mel seemed to notice George for the first time. B knew the Grande Mistress could tell at a glance that George was not a witch.

The other witch inspectors gathered around Madame Mel. They spoke in whispers, pointing to the vat of milk chocolate.

"We need to close down this wing of the factory temporarily to continue our health inspection," Madame Mel announced. "We have a more detailed analysis to perform. Everyone must leave."

"B, why don't you and George and Trina wait for me in the lobby," Mr. Cicely said. "I'll stay and help the, er, health inspectors."

B and her friends left the dipping room, but they didn't go far. As soon as they were past the glass doors, they gathered in a huddle.

I think Madame Mel suspects foul play," B whispered. "She thinks something's wrong with the milk chocolate!"

"Well, that's what I've been saying all along," George said. "I don't see why your dad needed Madame Mel to tell him that."

"No, but do you see? It's not the white chocolate, or the dark. It's not a problem with the recipe. I think Madame Mel believes someone added something to the milk chocolate. And you know who that must be?"

Trina shrugged. "No, who?"

"Jason Jameson!" B said.

"No way! How could he have done it?" Trina asked.

"He was here. His dad owns the company that supplied the fruit. There was some accident where the lights went out, and Jason was near the machine, trying to snitch a chocolate."

Trina sneezed. The overhead lights flickered. "But why would he try to eat a piece if he had put something bad in?"

"Oh, no," B said. "Trina, you're starting to get sick, too!"

"B, I really don't think Jason could have pulled off something this big," George said. "It's a magical sickness. You said so yourself. How could Jason cause that?"

"Who knows how magical illnesses are caused?" B said. "It could be anything. Look, I'm positive Jason was behind it somehow. We've got to get back inside there to look for clues. The others don't realize what a no-good ratfink Jason is. They won't know what to look for like we do."

"Well, we can't just go in there," George said. "Unless you two can make us invisible or something."

Trina and B exchanged glances. Yes, they were both witches, but there were limits to what they could safely do. They weren't that far along yet in their training.

"What if," Trina said slowly, "we made ourselves as small as mice?"

"Hmmm." B considered this. "Why not? Yeah, why not? That could work!"

"If you say so," George said, shrugging. "I don't see what's the big difference. Invisible, miniature . . ."

"C'mon, let's hurry," B said. She grabbed George's sleeve, and, concentrating hard, spelled "M-I-N-I-A-T-U-R-E."

She watched in wonder as George began to shrink, then felt a tinge of dismay as his size grew larger again. But wait a minute . . . He wasn't growing *larger*! It was B who was changing. She'd begun to shrink. Soon they were no taller than the electric outlet plugs along the walls. Trina was a giant!

Then they heard her world-famous singing voice booming in their tiny ears.

"Oh, I wanna be small, small, small,
Sneak into that room and hear it all!"

Trina was a singing witch. B always got a kick out of her pop-music-styled spells. But she wondered, with Trina starting to come down with this magical malady affecting all the other witches who'd eaten Fabulous Fruits, would her spells work?

Apparently this one did, for soon the lead singer of the Black Cats was the size of a cat's favorite snack.

"Let's go," B said. "We can climb through the

little gap between the swinging doors, then find a place to hide."

"How long will these spells last?" George asked. His voice sounded a little squeaky.

"Not sure," B said. "So we'd better hide behind a machine or something, just in case we get big again."

It was a scary business, dodging around the gigantic shoes and hurdling the fat electric cords that snaked along the floor. The witches' voices, high up above, seemed both loud and distant. At last they found what seemed like a safe place. They peered around behind a rack of unused Fabulous Fruit containers at Madame Mel and her emergency committee, with B's dad hovering close by. Globules of floating milk chocolate hovered above a strange magical device Madame Mel held up high. She whispered spell after spell, and at last a little puff of sparkly blue vapor rose from the chocolate samples. She snagged a sample of it in a test tube, added a vial of powder to it, and gave it a swirl. There was a small pop, and the blue mixture went up in smoky flames.

The witches all looked at each other.

"As I suspected," Madame Mel said, putting her instruments away. "There can be no further doubt. There's nothing wrong with the equipment or the recipe. This chocolate," she said with a meaningful look around the whole room, "was poisoned."

Chapter 9

"But who?" B's dad cried. "But how? Who could have done this? Who would want to?"

Madame Mel peered at him through her purple specs. "What about the factory workers? Everyone employed here has access to the chocolate, correct? Whoever did this slipped the poison right into the vat."

B's dad paced the floor. "Yes, but . . . they've all been here for years. They're practically family." He raked his scalp once more. His hair stood straight up. "I can't believe it. If you'd said that some spy from Pluto Candies had smuggled in something, I could have believed that. They'd do anything to sabotage Enchanted Chocolates. But nobody here had any ties to Pluto Candies. I'm sure of it."

Madame Mel snapped her fingers and her lab getup changed back into her regular magical robes. All her emergency committee did likewise. George's jaw dropped at the sight of Madame Mel's crazy blue hair and her long colorful robes covered head to toe in tinkling silver charms.

"It would have to be a witch, wouldn't it?" B's dad asked. "Since only witches are getting sick. Someone with magical knowledge must have done this, right?"

Madame Mel tucked her instruments into pockets on her shimmery robes. "Not necessarily," she said. "There have been cases where nonwitches have accidentally formed very potent brews and poisons. It's too soon to rule anything or anyone out yet."

Mr. Cicely raked his fingers through his hair for the umpteenth time.

"If you're sure it couldn't be any of your employees," Madame Mel said, "then what about the guests who were here at the dipping debut?"

B's dad pulled a photo from his briefcase. "This was taken yesterday."

Madame Mel frowned at the picture. "Odd," she said. "The only person there I can see with a history of incidents such as these is Doug Bishop."

B gasped. It was only a mouse-size gasp, but it was enough to make Madame Mel turn. George and Trina dragged B behind the shelves and out of sight.

Mr. Bishop! Her English teacher and magical tutor? He'd never do something like this.

Would he?

"I can't believe Madame Mel suspects Mr. Bishop," Trina whispered.

"Maybe it was the song he sang?" George suggested. "You know how songs are spells for Trina. Maybe Mr. Bishop is that way, too?"

"This investigation is far from complete," Madame Mel said. "In the meantime, production and distribution of Fabulous Fruits must be halted completely. We don't want any other witches getting sick. And, though I'm sure this goes without saying, I must ask everyone here to do all they can to keep this mysterious illness, and the investigation into it, top secret."

B's dad nodded. "I'll put a security lockdown on this entire wing as soon as we walk out," he said. "That will seal off the area. Not even a fly could get in or out after that."

"Perfect," Madame Mel said. She nodded to the rest of her team. "Time to get back."

They spoke their traveling spells and vanished. B's dad went around the room shutting things off and putting things away.

"Did you two hear that?" B whispered. "Dad's putting a lockdown on this wing. That means if we don't get out right now, we'll be stuck in here!"

"But if we return to our normal sizes, he'll see us," Trina said.

"And he'll know that I overheard everything," George added.

B gulped. "Then our only chance," she said, "is to hitch a ride. Come on!"

Mr. Cicely's shoes were nearly at the door by the time the mouse-size friends caught up with him. George was about to take a chance on the cuffs of his pants when B noticed her father's briefcase parked beside the door. "In here!" she whispered as loudly as she dared. One by one they vaulted into the compartment on the side of the bag intended for water bottles.

And not a moment too soon. The briefcase rose into the air and began swinging back and forth. No amusement park ride was ever so turbulent. Trina, whose sneezes inside the bag transformed a pen into a miniature bass guitar, lay curled up in the bottom of the compartment, groaning with nausea. B climbed over George and scrambled to the top of the compartment as a lookout. At the end of the corridor she could just make out the door to the lobby. Then she realized the new danger they faced. If her dad reached the lobby and found they weren't there, he might get suspicious. On the other hand, if they jumped out now, it was a long way to fall.

Fortune intervened, and B's dad set down his bag before opening the door. B and George jumped out, dragging Trina with them. Her sneezes had changed the color of her jacket from black to lemon yellow.

"R-E-T-U-R-N," she spelled, thinking hard about herself and George at their normal sizes. The ceiling rushed to meet them, but fortunately their bodies stopped expanding at just the right time.

Trina was not so lucky. She'd had just enough magic left to shrink herself. But now her face was covered with purple spots, and her song attempts wobbled off-key and didn't even come close to rhyming.

"What's happening to me, B?" she squeaked in a thin, tinny mouse voice. "What if I'm stuck like this forever?"

On the other side of the lobby wall B could hear her father asking Janika, "Any sign of the kids?"

B got down on one knee. "Don't worry, Trina," she said. "We'll figure it out. For now, come with me." She held out a hand, and Trina climbed into B's palm. B slipped her friend into the pocket of her sweatshirt and hurried with George back into the lobby.

"Here we are!" she said. "Just showing George around a bit."

"Where's Trina?" B's dad said.

"Oh. She had to leave," said B.

Apparently her dad was too preoccupied to think hard about this. "We need to leave, too. Come on, you guys, I'll drive you home."

In the car, B buckled her seat belt carefully, so as not to squash Trina. From within the folds of her sweatshirt she heard a teensy mouse-size sneeze. The squirters on the windshield began to spray.

"That's odd," Mr. Cicely said, wiggling the lever to turn the squirters off.

"Well, this car needs a good wash," B said, her heart pounding.

"Ah-choo!"

The radio turned on, and a Black Cats song began to play. B's father gave her a funny look through the rearview mirror. B realized that he suspected she was using magic recklessly, right in front of George. Uh-oh.

"Boy, that remote control of yours sure works great," B said loudly to George.

"That *what* of mine?"

"You know," B said, elbowing him. "That remote control you ordered online that can turn anything on? Like the radio of our car, just now?"

"Oh. Right," George said, catching on. "Yeah, it's pretty amazing."

"You'll have to show it to me sometime, George," B's dad said. "Oh, there's my phone."

B's dad's Crystal Ballphone began to ring. The ringtone was the jingle to Fabulous Fruits.

"Hello?"

B recognized her mother's voice, but she couldn't quite make out what she was saying.

"Oh, Stella, honey, I'm so sorry to hear that

you've *caught Dawn's cold,*" Mr. Cicely said loudly. "As soon as B and George and I get home, I'll come fix you some . . . turkey soup."

You mean chicken soup, B thought. *Nice try, Dad, trying to sound normal.* Any sick witch would prefer eel soup.

"Ah-ah-choo!"

The overhead lights snapped on, but B's dad didn't even notice. The car pulled into B's driveway.

"Hate to say this, George, but you'd better not come over today," B's dad said. "Sounds like we've got a bad sickness going through the family. Wouldn't want you catching it."

"No problem," George said, grinning. "Hope everybody feels better soon."

"Me, too," B's dad said. "Me, too."

B walked George across the lawn to his own house. Once they reached George's yard they hid behind some bushes and pulled Trina out of B's pocket. Poor Trina! She looked awful. Her face was covered with tiny pinprick-size purple spots. It only took one look to know her magic was completely gone. It was up to B to restore her to her proper size.

"R-E-T-U-R-N," she said. But the spell didn't work this time.

"N-O-R-M-A-L."

Nope.

"G-R-O-W."

"E-X-P-A-N-D."

"Careful, B," Trina piped up. "I don't want to end up any bigger than I'm supposed to be."

"Apparently there's no danger of that," B said. She was beginning to feel anxious. Was there some rule about witches not being able to reverse other witches' spells? If so, she'd never heard it before.

She thought hard about Trina. She pictured her carrying her plaid backpack down the hall, whipping a pillow at B during a sleepover, doing her dance moves in the flashing lights of a Black Cats concert.

"K-A-T-R-I-N-A," she spelled. B could swear she heard a little riff of bass guitar, then, poof! Trina appeared before them both, just the right size.

"That was weird," Trina said. *"Ah-choo!"* She pulled the hood of her jacket up over her face and took out her Ballphone to call her chauffeur.

"Get some rest," B advised. "And, I know it

sounds nasty, but you could always try chewing pages of a rhyming dictionary to get rid of the spots."

"Tell me you're joking." Trina groaned. "Will I ever get my magic back?"

"I'm sure you will," B said. "We're going to get to the bottom of this. I promise."

B said good-bye to her friends and ran home. The kitchen was in an uproar. Her mom sat wrapped in a blanket in a rocking chair at one end. Every time she sneezed, the blender started blending onions with strawberries or the frying pan started scrambling eggs with butterscotch chips.

"My ingredients!" B's mom wailed. "My deluxe cookware! Don't let the eggs burn onto the pan, B."

B tried not to smile. She turned the heat off on the stove and moved the hot pan to the sink. For now, at least, her mom was more concerned about her kitchen than her magic.

Dawn dragged herself into the room and sank into a kitchen chair. She wore a long fuzzy bathrobe and still kept most of her head and face covered by a scarf. But it didn't hide the huge purple blisters on her nose.

"Oh, Dawn!" B cried. "Your skin!"

"Don't remind me."

"Have you tried dictionary pages?"

Dawn stuck out her tongue. B found the old dictionary on the counter and ripped out a few pages from the "S" section, for "sister."

B's dad kicked off his shoes and sat next to his wife, holding her hand. "Madame Mel is on the case, working on a solution to the mystery," he said. "I'm sure the M.R.S. will announce a remedy soon."

"They'd better," B's mom said. "Otherwise we'll starve."

B's heart broke, seeing her family feeling so rotten, with all their magic gone. For a witch, losing your magic was like losing your right hand. B couldn't help being grateful that she, alone, knew that fruit and chocolate didn't belong together. At least now she still had magic to help take care of her family, not to mention solve this mystery. And solve it she would. Madame Mel suspected Mr. Bishop — B could scarcely credit that idea, but to be fair she'd have to test every theory. Meanwhile, she was still convinced that Jason Jameson was responsible for all the trouble. She was determined to find out how.

Chapter 10

The next day, during English class, B found it hard to concentrate on Mr. Bishop's lesson. She kept trying to imagine what Madame Mel might have meant by Mr. Bishop's "history of incidents," like poisoning the entire witching community. If he was such a threat, why did they let him teach students?

B decided to confront him directly. For this, she knew, she should be alone. So as soon as the bell rang, she whispered to Trina and George, "I need to talk to Mr. Bishop. I've got to find out what he knows. Why don't you guys keep an eye on Jason and see what he's up to? I'll meet you in the cafeteria."

"Okay, B," George said, "but do you remember what the banana said to the monkey?"

B blinked. *What on earth?* "No, what did the banana say?"

George grinned. "Nothing," he said. "Bananas can't talk."

Oh, toads.

"What has that got to do with anything?" Trina shouldered her backpack, looking thoroughly confused.

"Just George being George," B said. "And I know when Jason is being Jason. He's up to something. I can smell it! So keep an eye on him."

Trina, whose spots and sneezing had cleared up, but was still looking pale and tired, nodded. "Okay, B," she said. "We'll watch him. But remember, I can't do anything, er, you know, special if we do find a clue."

Meaning magical. B sighed. Poor Trina.

"Just watch him," B said. "I'll be there soon, and then we'll make a plan."

Mr. Bishop called over from where he was tidying the papers on his desk. "Everything okay, B, George?" he asked. "You feeling okay, Trina? You look a little under the weather."

"I've had better days," Trina said. "See you tomorrow." And she and George left the classroom. B went over to Mozart's cage and lifted the lid. Mr.

Bishop's classroom hamster, who had shared some magical adventures with B in the past, hopped into her outstretched hand.

B stroked his soft fur and tried to think of the best way to bring up the delicate subject of Mr. Bishop's possible guilt, but her magical tutor beat her to the punch.

"So, B," he said, sitting down on the desk in front of her, "you didn't poison the witching world the other day, did you?"

B gasped. "Me?" *Why does everybody always suspect me?* "I was going to ask you the same question!"

Mr. Bishop started with surprise. "Me? You think I might have done it?" He twisted the tip of his pointy beard.

Mozart could sense B was upset. He nuzzled his head against her palm.

"I would never do anything to make people sick," B said. "I can't believe you think I might."

Mr. Bishop smiled. "Don't be upset. I know you wouldn't mean to hurt anyone. But, maybe, did you brew up a potion to make the chocolates more delicious? Something like that, to help your dad with the launch of Fabulous Fruits? If you tell me what you used, I could probably brew up an antidote."

"I swear I didn't do anything magical," B said. "Madame Mel said you were the only witch she knew there with a history of causing mischief like this." Whoops! She probably shouldn't have said it out loud.

He threw back his head and laughed. "She said that, did she? Hilarious!"

"I don't see what's so funny about it," B said. "My whole family has lost their magic from this sickness. I'm the only one who can still make spells, because I never tried the nasty chocolate fruity junk."

"Not a fan of Fabulous Fruits?" Mr. Bishop wiped his eyes, still shaking with laughter.

"Well? Is it true that you have a history of things like this?"

"Oh, I may have gotten into some mischief when I was younger — *much* younger — but nothing major," he said. "I'm not the potion poisoner you're looking for."

"Well, neither am I," B said.

Mr. Bishop studied B for a minute. "Fair enough," he said.

B poured a few hamster pellets into her palm to feed to Mozart.

"And anyway," she went on, "how do you know you're not? What about that jingle you sang? It rhymed. How do you know it didn't work some kind of spell? Like Trina's singing magic? Which, incidentally, is gone now, too."

Mr. Bishop got up off the desk. "You worry too much, B," he said. "I know how to sing a song without making dozens of people sick. Rest assured that the M.R.S. is working hard on this, and I'm doing all I can to help." He went back to his desk and began sorting through piles of student work, as if it were the most everyday thing in the world, but B got the feeling that Mr. Bishop was more worried about the magical epidemic than he was letting on. She gave Mozart a kiss, placed him back in his cage, shouldered her backpack, and headed for the door.

"Don't forget, we've got a tutoring session after school today, B," Mr. Bishop called. "See you then."

Chapter 11

B walked slowly toward the cafeteria. So, it wasn't Mr. Bishop who'd done it. She felt certain he wasn't lying. He was as anxious to solve the mystery as she was. That left Jason Jameson where he'd always been, at the top of B's list of suspicious characters. But it wasn't enough to accuse him just because he was a known sneak. B needed facts: means, motive, and opportunity.

She entered the lunch line and ordered a sandwich without even checking to see what was in it. Trina and George weren't seated at their usual table. B scanned the lunchroom for her friends. She nearly dropped her bottle of chocolate milk back into the cooler when she caught sight of Trina sitting opposite Jason, chatting and smiling like they were old friends. Then Jason rose, returned his tray, and left the cafeteria. George, whom B had just located peering out from a janitor's closet, followed after him, staying focused on his target like a shark trailing its prey. What on earth was going on?

B joined Trina at the lunch table and sat in the seat Jason Jameson had just vacated.

"What's up, Trina?" B took a bite of her sandwich, which turned out to be a tuna melt. "Ugh! H-A-M, A-N-D, S-W-I-S-S," she whispered, watching her sandwich closely. "Ah. That's better. H-O-N-E-Y, M-U-S-T-A-R-D. Perfect."

"Lucky," Trina said. "It's not so easy to sing a sandwich. Even if I did have my magic."

"They'll find a cure," B said, reaching over to squeeze her friend's hand. "I know Madame Mel can do it, as soon as they figure out what caused the sickness. So, why on earth were you having lunch with Jason?"

Trina made a face. "Just following your orders to investigate him."

"Really?" B said. "What's George doing?"

Trina scraped the last of her pudding from its cup. "Well, we had different points of view on how to investigate. I thought the best way to learn what

Jason was up to would be to talk to him, but George didn't trust Jason. He wanted to follow him instead." She crumpled her pudding cup. "So we split up."

"Hm," B said. She wasn't sure whose strategy she liked better, but two strategies might be better than one. "Did you learn anything?"

"You bet," Trina said. "For one thing, I'm certain that Jason's got some mischief planned for today, after school."

B swallowed a big bite of ham and Swiss. This sounded promising. "How do you know?"

"Jason's such a phony. Remember how he treated me so rotten when I first moved here? And then, when everyone found out I was in the Black Cats, he was fawning all over me, trying to get invited to my house or to ride in the car?"

B nodded. How could she forget?

"Well, I figured if I invited him to come over to hear a new track from the Black Cats, that would be an irresistible opportunity for him, and maybe he'd let down his defenses so I could ask him more questions."

"Jumping jinxes," B said. "You actually invited Jason Jameson to your house?"

"Yeah, but get this," Trina said, leaning closer. "He said *no*."

B was staggered. Jason Jameson turned down a private invitation to the Black Cats' lead singer's mansion, and a private screening of their newest music? Cats fans would give their front teeth for such a chance. Next Trina would say the sky was falling.

"He said he had chess club at the town library, right after school," Trina said. "So I said, no problem, come on over after that. But he still said no. He had something to do after chess club that couldn't wait. And he wouldn't say what."

"That's really strange," B said. "You'd make a really good detective."

"Or a spy," Trina said. "Being a spy sounds more glamorous. So, are you going to meet me after school at the library to do a little spying on this chess club of Jason's?"

"Wish I could," B said. "I've got magic tutoring right after school with Mr. Bishop. But when that's done I could meet you there. Probably Jason would still be in his chess club."

"Works for me," Trina said. "Meet you outside the library, whenever you can get there."

B found George heading toward their gym class. "Hey, guess what, George?" she said. "Trina thinks Jason's planning something sneaky for this afternoon."

George removed his glasses and polished them on the bottom of his Wilmington Warlocks jersey. "Could be important," he said. "But I found something a little more concrete when I followed him out of lunch."

"Really? What?"

"Saw him opening his locker," George explained. "On the top shelf were a handful of Fabulous Fruits, plain as day, in a clear sandwich bag."

"That's weird," B said. "Saving them for later?"

"If he just wanted to eat them, they'd be gone by now," George said. "He must have some kind of plan for them."

"That's true," B said, nodding. "I knew it! Jason's up to something. But what?"

"Only one way to find out," George said, "and that's keeping Jason under surveillance."

"That's just what Trina suggested we do after school," B said.

At this, George's face fell. B was puzzled. She couldn't think what would have made him unhappy.

"Are you okay, George?" B asked.

"Yeah."

They went into the gym and sat on the bleachers to wait for Coach Lyons. George still seemed pretty glum.

"You *sure* you're okay?"

George let out a sigh. "It's just . . ." He lowered his voice. "It's just, you and Trina, it's so weird. . . ."

B felt a flutter of worry. "You found a great clue, George." She put a hand on his arm. "Don't you like Trina?"

"No, no, that's not it." George took a deep breath. "My two closest friends turn out to be witches. You guys can do these amazing things, and what am I? Boring."

B couldn't have been more surprised if her own face started breaking out in purple spots. She never saw this coming. Poor George!

"You? Boring? You've got to be kidding me! George, you're . . . I mean, you've been my best friend since forever. You're not boring; you're hilarious."

George waved this away. "Come on. You know my jokes are lame. You've got all these *powers*."

"Your jokes are *not* lame." Other kids started looking over at them, so B lowered her voice again to a whisper. "Okay. Maybe they are lame. But you've got lame jokes down to an art. George, you're the smartest kid in this school, and the best athlete, and the best friend a kid could have. Those are powers, too. I wish I had more of them!"

George wasn't convinced. "Lots of kids are smart or athletic. But you can just spell words, and Trina can just sing songs, and make things happen," George said.

"No, she can't," B said. "Not now. Her magic is gone. And if we don't find a cure for this illness, a lot of witches will lose their magic and stop being witches."

For a second, B imagined losing her own magic. It felt like losing her ability to breathe. Magic was so much a part of who she was now. She felt a new sympathy for how George must be feeling.

"Don't feel bad, George," B said. "There's no way we can solve this mystery without you. We need your help. Magical or not."

George looked up at B from under his curly hair. A little smile broke through. "I'm sorry," George said. "I don't mean to complain about not having magic."

"It's okay," she said. "Just don't forget, every kid in this school wishes they were more like you." She smiled. "Including me."

Coach Lyons came into the gym, late as usual, blowing his whistle and barking orders. He made the kids count off into teams, which meant B and George got separated.

"I'll meet you at the library at four o'clock," George said. "Don't worry. We're going to solve this mystery. I'm on the case."

Chapter 12

B already knew what she wanted to learn that afternoon when she arrived in Mr. Bishop's classroom for her magical tutoring session.

"How hard is it to turn yourself invisible, Mr. Bishop?"

Mr. Bishop poked his horn-rimmed glasses back up his nose. "Well, now. Invisibility. That's challenging, especially for beginner witches, and I imagine that even with your spelling brand of magic, it'll test your abilities."

"Why?" B said. "What's so hard about it?"

"For starters, like all magic, it requires tremendous focus. You have to really train your mind not to wander and float from this subject to that. You have to be very quiet in your mind, and quiet in your body, too."

"Huh? Quiet in your body?"

Mr. Bishop laughed. "I know it sounds funny, but that's the best analogy I can think of. If you don't want someone to hear you, what do you do? You go as quiet as you can. If you don't want someone to see you, you have to, er, quiet the image of yourself. Make yourself fade out. Be so still, so physically and mentally still, that it won't take much more work for the magic to make you just disappear. Does that make sense?"

B considered for a moment. "I think so. It sounds simple, but I'll bet it's hard."

"Like most things. But it's not just the spells. You know that. Magic is more than hocus-pocus."

"Rhymes with 'focus,'" B pointed out.

"Ha. Right. I'll bet that, with practice, you'll be able to do it for a few minutes, at the most. Even very experienced witches can't keep up invisibility for long. Ready to try it?"

"Sure."

Mr. Bishop locked his classroom door. "Okay. Get yourself as still as you can, and as calm, then spell 'invisible.'"

B leaned against the back wall of the classroom

and tried to relax. She imagined her appearance fading. She breathed slowly and quietly. "I-N-V-I-S-I-B-L-E," she whispered.

And she disappeared!

For a second.

Then she disappeared again.

Her body seemed to be turning on and off, like a lamp when a little kid is playing with the switch. Watching herself disappear was fun, and she felt a little drop in the pit of her stomach each time, like a dip on a roller coaster. But try as she might, she couldn't get the effect to last.

"Not bad, not bad," Mr. Bishop said. "It can take years of practice to develop the concentration to disappear even once. You're off to a great start."

"But I want to go totally invisible," B said. "Think how useful that would be!"

"Are you planning a career as a jewel thief?" Mr. Bishop smiled. "All right. I'll add a spell to help you this time. You perform your spell again, and then I'll add mine, and I think that'll do the trick."

B spelled "invisible" again, and Mr. Bishop said,

Vanishing's no easy art.

B needs a boost. She's done her part."

And, *poof*! B disappeared!

She bent forward to look through where her torso ought to be and saw the wall behind her. This was so fun. But just as she was about to say so to Mr. Bishop, rushing breezes swept into the room. Madame Mel appeared, flanked by a squadron of large, tough-looking witches in sunglasses. They wore tall, heavy boots, and uniform robes with the letter "D" emblazoned across their backs. Two of them immediately checked the doors, closed the blinds, and examined the room. B had to hold her breath when one of them passed within inches of her.

With a flash, B realized who they were. They had to be the Dismantle Squad!

A burly witch with a brush cut, standing next to Madame Mel, said, "Doug T. Bishop. You are under suspicion of using a potion as a poison, and tainting a large batch of chocolate for the purpose of making large numbers of witches seriously ill and compromising their magic. As a suspect in this most serious crime against the witching community, we request you now come with us. You are advised that, should you refuse to come peacefully, we will be forced to apprehend you." At this, the other Dismantle Squad members folded their arms across their chests.

Jumping jinxes! It was all B could do to stay calm and invisible. This was serious! That Dismantle Squad was scary. She'd never seen this side of the M.R.S. before.

"I'll come with you," Mr. Bishop said loudly, "because I'm happy to cooperate. I haven't done any-thing wrong" — here two Dismantle Squad members each grabbed one of his wrists — "and no one should worry about me, or try to do anything to help me. I'm innocent, and everything will be fine in the end."

Madame Mel's forehead crinkled with puzzle-ment. "A moving speech, Doug," she said, "but it will be up to the Magical Rhyming Society's Council of Justice to determine innocence or guilt after the Dismantle Squad has completed its investigation. Let's go."

Mr. Bishop turned toward where B stood and winked at her. She looked down and saw her sneakers beginning to flicker into view and tried not to gasp.

"Something in your eye?" Madame Mel asked Mr. Bishop.

"Er, yes," he said. Then he added:

"Make my last spell a little bit stronger.

Stretch its effects out a little bit longer!"

B looked down again. Her feet had vanished.

"What, exactly, was your last spell?" Madame Mel said, tapping the toe of her high-heeled boots.

"Oh, just something to make sure my hamster, Mozart, gets fed and watered every day, without me needing to worry. Who knows how long I'll be gone?"

The chief Dismantler, or so he seemed to be, uttered a staccato spell, and the whole group whisked off to the M.R.S.

B blew out her breath. "V-I-S-I-B-L-E," she spelled, thinking about her body, and she popped back into focus. Then she sank into Mr. Bishop's desk chair.

Mr. Bishop! Arrested! She was sure that he was innocent. And Jason Jameson, she was even surer, was *not*. She had to solve this crime and prove who the real poisoner was. She set off running down the hall and out the door of the school, to the library and chess club, as fast as she could go.

Chapter 13

B found Trina and George perched in the lower branches of a tree in a park across the street from the library.

"Nice stakeout, you two," B said. "Is Jason still in there?"

"Ssh!" Trina hissed. "Here he comes now! Hide, B!"

B crouched behind a monument until George gave her the signal. He and Trina jumped down from their tree, and B rose to follow. Jason headed toward Main Street.

"We can't let him see us," B said. "I have an idea. D-I-S-G-U-I-S-E."

Trina's long dark hair went short and blond, and her black jeans and jacket turned into a frilly purple dress.

"Yuck!" Trina yelped. "I can't be seen in this!"

"Precisely," B said. "*You* won't be. He won't recognize you." She turned to George and began laughing. "Jumping jinxes! Look at you!"

Tall, athletic George had gotten at least six inches shorter, and his Wilmington Warlocks jersey had turned into a Montgomery Miracles sweatshirt. He plucked at it with his much smaller hands. "I can't wear this thing!" he said. "I'll die of embarrassment. Nobody backs the Montgomery Miracles. Nobody!"

B giggled.

"Look at yourself, B," Trina said. B looked down to see cowboy boots where her sneakers had been and a rhinestone-studded vest over her shirt.

"Howdy, pardner," George said. "C'mon, Jason's getting away. Let's go!"

They followed him, Trina on one side of the road, and B and George on the other. Once or twice Jason paused and looked over his shoulder, but Trina, B, and George were ready. They paid no attention to him, and just blended in with the other pedestrians. Apparently satisfied, Jason moved on.

He turned a corner and headed toward an industrial park. Trina jogged across the street to join B and George. They peered around the corner until they saw which factory building he was heading toward.

B's jaw dropped. "Pluto Candies?!"

"Come on!" George said. "He's going to the back of the building. Let's run around the other way. We can hide in those shrubs."

Trina and B were no match for George's speed. They ran after him as best they could, out of breath.

"He tapped on a window," George whispered. "Look! It's opening!"

A stout woman with a very red nose and cheeks greeted Jason briefly.

B, George, and Trina looked at each other. *"Mrs. Pluto?"* they whispered.

Sure enough, the woman at the window had her smiling, rosy, much prettier-looking face printed on every Pluto box of chocolate sold. In real life, Mrs. Pluto's "rosy" cheeks were lobster red, her stringy hair slipped out from her bun, and her eyes were small and piglike.

She and Jason spoke for a moment, then Jason handed her a small baggie. She took it and disappeared.

"Those are the Fabulous Fruits I saw in his locker," George whispered. "So that's why he swiped them. Why, that dirty little traitor!"

Mrs. Pluto reappeared at the window and handed Jason two huge boxes of Pluto Candies. He stuffed them into his backpack and left — but not before he'd taken a double handful of chocolates from one of the boxes and stuffed them in his mouth.

"Just like that! The formula for Fabulous Fruits, sold for a few boxes of crummy Pluto Candies," B said. "Wait till I tell my dad!"

"Look at it this way," George said. "In a week or so, they'll be in the stores, so she could have copied the recipe then. Jason's actually done you a favor. He's given them the bad candy. If their scientists try to analyze what they find in those chocolates, they'll end up very confused."

"Excellent point, George," B said. "Still, I want to know what's going on in there. Maybe Pluto Candies gave Jason a poison to drop into the chocolate mixer at the Fabulous Fruits launch, and that caused . . . something."

"I agree," George said. "We've got to find a way to get inside."

"Don't you just want more chocolate?" Trina said, poking George.

"Are you kidding? I wouldn't eat Pluto Candies if they were the last chocolates on earth. I'm no Jason Jameson."

"Anyway, I don't see how any of us can get in," Trina said. "I saw guards just inside the front door. We'll never make it past Mrs. Pluto's security. Even Jason had to be all sneaky and tap on her window."

"If I were a witch like you two, it would be easy," George said. He kicked at a weed in the bushes.

"Magic doesn't make everything easy, you know," Trina said. "And anyway, you've eaten so much Fabulous Fruit that if you were a witch, you sure wouldn't be one now. You'd be covered in purple spots!"

B felt sick to her stomach, watching her best friends arguing.

"Hey, guys," B said. "Let's not get upset. I worked with Mr. Bishop today on invisibility spells. It's not easy, but maybe I can make us all invisible for a few minutes. Then we can all sneak inside. But we'll have to be quick! The spell doesn't last long."

This silenced George and Trina. Then B had to work on silencing herself. Without Mr. Bishop's help she had barely made herself flicker, and now she proposed to turn three people invisible? What was she thinking? On the other hand, anything was better than listening to George and Trina argue.

Quiet body. Quiet mind.

"You sure you can do this, B?" Trina said.

"Yes." B wished she was as certain as she sounded.

"I-N-V—"

"I thought you said yesterday that invisibility was super-advanced magic," George said. "Remember? When I suggested it?"

"Yes, I remember," B said. "Guys! I really need to focus on this one. Give me a minute with no interruptions, okay?"

Can I do this? Can I pull it off? She thought of

her family, sneezing, covered in spots, and unable to form spells. *This is important. We've got to get in there to find out what's going on.*

B grabbed George's and Trina's hands. "I-N-V-I-S-I-B-L-E," she said.

Poof! All three of them disappeared!

"Whoa," George said, laughing. "This is the coolest thing that's ever happened to me."

"No time! Run!" B said. A delivery man was just approaching the back door to Pluto Candies. B and her friends hurried to get right behind him, bumping into each other's invisible arms and legs a little on the way.

A security guard opened the door. "Afternoon, Al," he said. And while he signed for the package, B, Trina, and George hunkered down low and tiptoed past him.

They sprinted down the corridor and entered the first production room they came to. "This way, this way," B kept whispering, trying to keep her friends together. B recognized candy-making equipment like the kinds at Enchanted Chocolates, only these machines looked old and rusty. They creaked as they moved. Cobwebs hung thickly from the corners of the rooms, and the floors looked like they hadn't seen a mop in a long time.

A worker came into the room in dirty overalls, carrying a crate of peanuts. "I don't know, Boss, these peanuts don't look so good. You sure we can still use 'em?"

"Covered in chocolate, no one'll know the difference," the boss said. Neither of them, B noted with a frown, wore a hairnet. By law, they should. "Dump 'em in the hopper, and we'll use these for the premium bridge mix."

"Uggh." B heard George groaning.

"Come on," she whispered. "Let's try another room."

Next was a chocolate-mixing room. Boxes of cocoa were being dumped into the gigantic vat along with buckets of cream and sugar. But there was a problem.

"This sugar's hard as a rock," a worker was saying as she whacked at it with a crowbar. "Fifty pounds of sugar brick."

"Must've gotten wet," another worker said. "The roof leaks back in the warehouse. I'll bet it got rained on. Here, I'll help you dump it in. The mixer blades will chop it up."

But they didn't chop it up. The mixing machine groaned to a halt.

"I can't watch this," George said.

"No wonder Enchanted Chocolates sells so much better," B said. Then she heard footsteps coming down the corridor. "Quick! Against the wall!"

She pressed herself flat against it and held her breath while Mrs. Pluto herself passed by. Could *she* be a witch? Of course there was no real way to know by looking, but the greasy apron, the angry-looking red face, and the mean glint in her eye seemed about as unmagical as you could get.

Just as Mrs. Pluto passed by, B caught sight of a glimmer of George, right next to her. They were fading into view already!

Mrs. Pluto paused, and turned to look back at where they stood. Faster than she'd ever spelled anything, B whispered, "I-N-V-I-S-I-B-L-E." George vanished once more.

Mrs. Pluto blinked, and rubbed her eyes. She stared at the spot where George had been. B held her breath, but Mrs. Pluto carried on walking.

As soon as she was out of sight, B turned toward where her friends were and gasped, "Come on, we've got to go."

"We haven't learned anything yet," George said. "I want to check out this room."

"No. Come on, now!"

B repeated her invisibility spell, and they ran back to the front lobby. Only the sound of their footsteps assured B that her friends were really following her. While the security guard watched his television screen, she took a chance, opened the door, and slipped out. Then she retreated back to the bushes where they'd started.

"We made it," she said to Trina, who was now fully visible. "Whew!" Then she froze. "Wait! Where's George?"

"He must still be inside," Trina said. "What do we do?"

"I'll go back for him," B said. "Maybe I can create a distraction to help him get out."

B marched to the front door. There, just behind the glass, sat the security guard, and behind him, making goofy faces, was a fully visible George. Oh, no.

B opened the door. The guard looked up. "Yeah? What do you want?"

She took a deep breath. "I'm doing a project for school on how my favorite candies are made," she said, "and I was wondering if I could have a tour of the factory." She tried to make eye contact with George, but he was too busy acting like an ape.

"No tours," the huge guard growled. He looked like he spent most of his extra time bodybuilding. George held up a pair of rabbit-ear fingers behind his head.

B caught George's eye and gave a tiny shake of her head.

He stopped. His face went pale as he looked down at himself and realized he was visible.

Chapter 14

The guard was still glowering at B.

"What's your problem, kid? Cat got your tongue? I said, no tours!"

B's heart thumped as George tried to edge around the guard's office. He bumped into a stack of film canisters marked SECURITY TAPE and sent them rolling across the floor.

The guard spun around in his chair. "Hey, how'd you get back there?" He leaped up and grabbed George by the collar. "Outta here!"

He shoved George and B out the door. "Nosy kids! Stay out. If you want to bother someone, go to Enchanted Chocolates. We're busy."

On the way back home, B told Trina and George about the Dismantle Squad capturing Mr. Bishop. They stopped in their tracks.

"Our English teacher's been *arrested*?" George said.

"I'm not sure," B said. "But it was pretty serious and official, all the same." She kicked at an acorn on the sidewalk. "I wish we'd figured out something at Pluto Candies, but we don't know any more now than we did before. I was so sure Jason Jameson was the poisoner! But what if he's nothing but a sneak?"

"You should never give Jason Jameson too much credit," George said. "He's not smart enough to find a way to poison witches. Even by accident."

Trina snapped her fingers. "Didn't you guys say that Jason was there with his dad at the dipping debut?" she said. "What if his dad's the poisoner?"

George and B exchanged glances. "Jason does seem like a chip off the old block," George said.

B nodded. "Good hunch, Trina. I'll mention it to my dad."

B found her parents both curled up under blankets on the couch. B's mom had a cup of eel broth and a box of tissues on her end table. Everyone had told her the sickness wasn't contagious, but she still hesitated before giving each of them a kiss.

"Dad. Mom. Mr. Bishop taught me an invisibility spell today at magic tutoring, and just when I was invisible, Madame Mel and the Dismantle Squad came and took Mr. Bishop away. They think he's the chocolate poisoner."

"You learned an invisibility spell, B?" her mother said. "That's nice."

"But, Mom!" B said. "Aren't you shocked by the news? It can't be Mr. Bishop!"

"We're not shocked, because we already knew," B's dad said, sipping his elm bark soda. "Madame Mel called to tell me. She's keeping me posted on the investigation, including their progress with suspects."

B's backpack fell to the floor. "Don't tell me you think Mr. Bishop actually did this!"

"Don't shout," her father said, wincing. "We both have whopping headaches."

B's mom opened her eyes wearily. "We certainly hope it's not Mr. Bishop who poisoned the chocolate. But we don't know anything for sure."

B sank into an easy chair. Her black cat, Nightshade, leaped into her lap, and B stroked him absentmindedly. All of this was beyond horrible. "What about that Mr. Jameson, the fruit guy?" she said. "His son Jason is the nastiest kid in school."

"He's a suspect, definitely," B's dad said, rubbing his temples. "But why would he want to sabotage one of his own accounts?"

"Guess what I discovered his son was doing today," B began, but she was interrupted by her dad's Crystal Ballphone ringing. He reached into his pocket with difficulty to pull it out.

"Hello?"

"Hello, Felix?" Madame Mel's distinct voice boomed through the speaker, loud enough for everyone to hear. "We're making some progress in our investigation."

"Oh?"

"Yes. Listen, can I stop by to fill you in?"

"Sure."

"Okay, see you soon."

And before B's dad could snap his phone shut and slide it back into his pocket, there she stood, in their living room. Even B, who was used to magical exits and entrances, was startled.

"Afternoon, folks," Madame Mel said, nodding to B and her parents. She handed B's dad a scroll of yellow parchment. "Official lab results are back. No question about it. The chocolate" — she peered ominously through her spectacles — "was poisoned by a potion."

B let this news sink in. It couldn't be Jason Jameson, then. Or his dad. They were both off the list. "That means . . ." she began.

"That means," Madame Mel took over, "that the poisoner is definitely one of us."

"But who would do that?" B said. "Why would a witch want to make other witches lose their magic?"

Madame Mel's face was grim. "I don't know," she said, "but when I find out . . ." She stopped herself, then patted B's mom on the shoulder. "Don't you worry," she said, "the medical lab is working night and day to find a remedy. Don't lose hope yet."

The next day at school B saw a smudge of chocolate on Jason Jameson's mouth in homeroom. After art class, she caught him pulling a fistful of chocolates out of his locker and stuffing them into his mouth.

Even if he wasn't the Fabulous Fruits poisoner, he was still a rotten snitch.

"Thought you weren't allowed to eat chocolate, Jason," she said. "Fruit is nature's candy, remember?"

"Mind your beeswax, Bumblebee," Jason sneered, reaching for another handful.

B was so angry, she practically saw spots. "I know what you did with the Fabulous Fruits you stole from me yesterday," she hissed. "You will never, ever be allowed into the Enchanted Chocolates factory again."

"What do I care?" Jason sneered. "Who needs your pathetic chocolate, when I've been promised a lifetime supply of Pluto Candies?"

"Serves you right, then," B said, "since apparently you love chocolate-covered dog food."

By the time they reached English class, Jason was looking sickly green, and walking stiffly with a stooped back. Mr. Bishop, as B had feared, wasn't there. A substitute teacher took his place, a scowly older woman who really needed to tweeze the whiskers on her chin.

"My name is Ms. Brewster," she said. "Your

teacher, Mr. Bishop, isn't feeling well. He's left instructions that you're to spend this class period in the library, reading."

The class gathered their things to file off to the library. Suddenly, Jason, clutching his stomach, ran to the sub and whispered in her ear. Her eyes grew wide, and she nodded. He bolted out the door.

"Serves him right for stealing chocolate," B muttered.

"And for eating so much Pluto Candy crud," George said.

"Without sharing," Trina added.

They all grinned.

Chapter 15

While Ms. Brewster read a magazine, B, George, and Trina commandeered a table in a secluded corner of the library. "This is perfect," B said. "We need a new plan of attack."

Trina drummed her fingers on the table. "What would an expert detective do?"

George passed around a bag of Enchanted Caramelicious Cremes. "Wouldn't they pretty much do what we've been doing? Search for clues, follow suspects?" He noticed Trina hesitate over taking a candy. "Don't worry," he said. "I bought them well before the potion incident."

"What else could we do?" B said. Her gaze fell on a shelf of books with blue stickers on the lower spine. "I know," she said. "Mystery novels! Let's each grab a few and browse through them. Maybe they'll give us ideas for how great detectives solve crimes."

They each took several books and began skimming through them.

Several minutes passed while they studied their books. Sherlock Holmes, Miss Marple, Nancy Drew, Amelia Peabody, Sam Spade, Hercule Poirot, Encyclopedia Brown. So many interesting detectives, but many strategies didn't fit their situation. For one thing, there were no fingerprints, no blood samples, no DNA to test, and not even any eyewitnesses.

Or were there?

"Here's a thought," George said. "In these old Agatha Christie novels, detectives liked to stage a reenactment of the crime. They gather together all the possible suspects, everybody who was involved, in the room where it all happened, and recreate the event."

"Why?" Trina said. "What good does that do?"

George flipped through more pages. But B could already see the advantages. "That's a brilliant idea," she said. "You get everyone together, talking about what they each saw . . . maybe they all saw different things, you know? Put it all together, and something becomes clear."

"Or maybe," George added, his thumb still in his book, "maybe, since the criminal is actually there, maybe they do or say something that proves they're guilty."

"What have we got to lose?" Trina said. "Do you think we could get everyone together?"

B thought a minute. "My dad could," she said, "if we can sell him on the idea."

Trina fished around in her backpack and handed B a slick, compact Crystal Ballphone. "Oh, man, Dawn would be green with envy if she saw this baby," B said.

"Call your dad, right now," Trina urged. "Ms. Brewster's not looking."

B dialed her father's office number.

"Hey, Dad," she said when he answered. "I have an idea."

And to B's astonishment, her dad loved it. He listened to B's entire explanation of why their plan might help, and agreed to call Madame Mel and ask her to bring Mr. Bishop and the mayor. They considered inviting Mr. Jameson, but after the Pluto

Candies affair, B's dad wasn't eager to welcome any Jamesons back into the factory. "Besides, B," he said, "the nonwitching world has no idea that there's a problem, and we certainly don't want to draw anyone's attention to that fact, or rumors might spread that would hurt the company. It was a potion that caused the trouble, so there really has to have been a witch involved, somehow."

They agreed to set up the reenactment for immediately after school, since B and George needed to be there. But when B, George, and Trina arrived at Enchanted Chocolates, B's dad pulled B aside.

"I'm sorry, B," he said. "I know we said George could come, because he was here at the dipping debut, but we're trying to catch a witch. The room will be full of witchy people talking about witchy subjects. We just can't have George there."

"Aw, Dad," B said. "What'll I tell him? There's no one who cares more about Enchanted Chocolates than George."

"I know that," B's dad said. "Tell him he can come back for a tour of the entire factory next week. I'll give him a coupon for a free package of the chocolate of his choice. But he can *not* come to this. That's final."

He left the room, and B broke the news to George. As she feared, George was crushed. "Can't you use your magic to get me in there somehow? Make me invisible?"

"You saw how long that lasted yesterday," B said.

"Make me mouse-size, then," he pleaded. "I can help! I know I can."

"But what if something goes wrong, George?" B said. "I'll get in such huge trouble. Madame Mel, Mr. Bishop, my dad . . . they're all going to be there."

George turned away. "Just another example of how I miss out because I'm not a witch."

B bit her lip. Did she dare try it? George had worked hard to help solve this crime. It wasn't fair that he should miss out now.

"M-I-N-I-A-T-U-R-E," she spelled, concentrating only on George. When he was done shrinking, a huge grin on his face, she dropped him in her sweat-shirt pocket.

Mr. Cicely returned to the lobby. "Time to get started, B. Trina, can you stand in for Mr. Jameson?"

They reached the Fabulous Fruits wing and changed into the protective white suits. Madame Mel and Mr. Bishop were both there, but they weren't really making eye contact with each other. That made B sad. They'd always seemed like such good old friends. Mr. Bishop looked bleary-eyed and rumpled, like he'd slept in his clothes and hadn't been able to shower or shave.

Mayor Cumberland swept into the room a few minutes later on a whirlwind of magical annoyance. He dabbed his nose with a tissue.

"Must we take time out for this spectacle?" he said. "It's not easy, holding a post at the M.R.S. and being mayor of the entire city! I have three meetings I'm missing to be here."

"That would have been quite a challenge, attending three meetings at once," Mr. Bishop observed. "You should be glad we've spared you that."

"Hmph," Mayor Cumberland said, sniffing. He blew his nose loudly. "And on top of everything, I'm terribly under the weather," he said. "Have been for days. The malady sweeping the magical community hasn't left me unscathed."

"I'm sorry to hear it, Mayor Cumberland," B's dad said. "And I do so much appreciate you taking the time to be here. We'll try to be as quick as we can. Madame Mel? Doug? B and Trina? If everyone's ready, let's begin."

Chapter 16

B moved toward the place she'd been standing when the lights went out. Then something jabbed her in the side. George! She'd almost forgotten he was in her pocket.

She ducked behind a machine and pulled him out so she could whisper to him.

"Put me on that conveyor belt," George said in his mouse voice. "I can climb up onto the main mixing vat without anybody seeing me. Then I'll be able to see everything that's going on."

"Okay, but good luck," B said. "And whatever you do, *don't* let anyone see you!"

George ran off, and B's eyes followed him nervously all the way up to his perch on the main mixer. No one, she was sure, had seen him.

"All right, folks," B's dad said. "Other than

dumping out the contaminated chocolate and replacing it with a fresh supply, and cleaning everything, nothing has changed in this room. It's the same as the day of the dipping debut. Does everyone remember where they were standing?"

"Well, when?" Mr. Bishop said. "Before the lights went out, or after?"

"Excellent point, Doug," B's dad said. "Let's begin with the assumption that the poisoner struck during the moment when the lights had gone out. It's not absolutely certain, but it seems the most probable."

"If there even was a poisoner," the mayor said. "You act as though it's a proven fact."

"A poisoned potion was added to the chocolate." Madame Mel's height made her tower over Mayor Cumberland. "That is a fact upon which I will stake my professional reputation."

"Of course, of course," the mayor said, cringing slightly.

"I remember where people were when the lights came back on," B said. "I remember, because I was paying close attention."

"That's odd, if you ask me," the mayor said. "Suggests a suspicious mind."

"Go on, B," Mr. Bishop said. "Tell us what you remember."

"You were standing here," she told her teacher. "By this machine. You'd just finished singing your song."

"*'Freshness with a triple dip,'*" Trina sang spontaneously, until Madame Mel frowned at her. "Er, sorry."

"And you, Mayor, were right next to Mr. Bishop." She tried to nudge the mayor into his spot, but he resisted.

"Now, Wallace," Madame Mel said. "We're here for a reenactment. Please cooperate."

"You, Dad, were over here by the switches with Mr. Jameson. So, Trina, you need to stand here by Dad."

"That means you could have flipped the switches yourself," Madame Mel observed.

"You're not suggesting that I'd poison my own chocolate, are you?" Mr. Cicely said.

Madame Mel's expression was cryptic. "Stranger things have happened."

B moved quickly to change the subject. "I was standing here," she said, "with my friend George." She gave him a quick glance to make sure he was still all right. "Jason Jameson, a nasty boy from my grade in school, was standing by the conveyor belt, waiting for fruit to come out so he could grab the first piece. . . ."

"And steal it," Mr. Cicely interrupted. Clearly, he hadn't gotten over this outrage.

"And eat it," B said. "I saw him pigging out. As soon as the lights came back on, I marched over to him to confront him, but I slipped in a puddle of blue potion!"

"Why didn't you say so then, B?" her father said. "We could have saved ourselves so much trouble!"

"Blue," Madame Mel mused. "Blue. What makes a potion blue? Hmm. I should call the alchemy department."

"How do you know it was potion, and not something else?" the mayor asked.

"Because it behaved like potion," she said. "It shimmered and swirled."

"B knows a potion when she sees one," Mr. Bishop said.

B snapped her fingers. "You saw it, too, didn't you, Mr. Bishop?" she said. "I remember now. You wiped it up with your handkerchief."

Conversation ceased as all eyes turned toward B's tutor. *Uh-oh.* B hadn't considered this. She remembered that right after the poisoning was discovered, she'd thought it was suspicious. Of course the others would now form the same conclusion.

"I did wipe up a blue potion," Mr. Bishop said calmly. "Frankly, since B was lying in a puddle of it, I thought it possible that she had made some secret potion, perhaps to try to help the chocolate taste better."

"You might have mentioned this sooner, Doug," Madame Mel said.

"I saw no point," he said, "since, upon talking with B, I felt certain she was innocent."

B couldn't help a little rush of pride. She was grateful she had her teacher's trust. She was just about to mention that after she tripped, Mr. Bishop and the mayor helped her up, and chocolaty handprints had been left all over her back. But she realized this would only heap more suspicion on her teacher.

"Does anyone have anything else to add?" Madame Mel said. "I thought not. Well, this has been interesting, to be sure, but unproductive. Thank you for coming. You may all go now."

"And high time, too," muttered Mayor Cumberland. "With any luck, I can still catch two of my meetings." He crossed the production floor, pausing for a heavy sneeze just as he passed by the main chocolate vat.

"Bless you," a tiny voice said.

B saw George cover his mouth with his tiny hand. Jumping jinxes!

Mayor Cumberland turned to B. "Did you hear something?"

"Just you, sneezing," B said. "I said, 'bless you.' "

The mayor looked puzzled. "That was you?" He turned around slowly, searching for another source. B breathed a sigh of relief when he didn't notice George, who had hidden himself behind a length of narrow steel pipe.

But when the mayor's gaze was again fixed on the exit, George leaped out from his hiding place, waving both hands in the air to get B's attention. He pointed both hands at the mayor.

The mayor? B studied him. He pulled a spotted red handkerchief from the pocket of his tweed jacket, unfolded it, and sneezed loudly once more.

And nothing happened!

No vats started churning, no dippers dipping, no conveyor belts whirring.

That was it!

Mayor Cumberland said he had the magical illness, but unlike when the other witches sneezed, nothing happened. Why would someone pretend to be sick?

B sidled over to the chocolate tank and leaned against it nonchalantly. George crept over and whispered in her ear.

"The mayor poured a thingy of sparkly liquid into the chocolate!"

"When, at the dipping debut?" B whispered back.

"No. Just now. Whoops!" George was so excited that he slipped into the vat.

"Are you okay?" B peeked in at him.

"I'm fine!" George said, treading chocolate. "I can climb out. Stop that mayor, now!"

B's dad shook hands with the other witches present, and B saw them begin to utter their traveling spells.

"Everyone, stop where you are!" B cried loudly.

Chapter 17

All eyes turned toward B. She felt her tongue go dry. She hated everyone staring at her and could feel the symptoms of stage fright coming on, fast.

"B, honey." B's dad raked his hand through his hair. "I know you're trying hard to help, but it's over, and we didn't learn anything." He turned to the others. "Sorry about that."

"It's not over," B said. She took a deep breath. She'd just have to speak for George. "I saw the mayor pour some potion into this vat of chocolate. Just now."

You could have heard a mouse sneeze in the Fabulous Fruits room.

Trina's eyes shone, but everyone else looked stunned.

"Mayor Cumberland?" B's dad said. "B, are you sure?"

"What a load of nonsense!" the mayor spluttered. "I didn't come here to be insulted by schoolgirls! Like I said, I'm very busy today and it's time I left. *Magical transport, whisk me . . ."*

"Hold on a moment, Wallace," Madame Mel said. "B has just made a very serious allegation against you. If what she says is true, then . . ."

"Well, of course it isn't true!" he snapped. "Why would I dump a potion into the chocolate, now or at any time?"

"I don't know," Madame Mel said. "Why would you?"

"I'm the minister of health," he said. "I'm not in the business of making people sick!"

"You're sick yourself, aren't you?" B asked.

"That's right," the mayor said. "I've been miserable ever since the dipping debut."

"You didn't seem miserable when you came to our house with Dr. Jellicoe that night," B said.

"That's true," B's dad agreed. He was starting to look rather differently at Mayor Cumberland.

"My symptoms came on later that night," insisted the mayor. *"Aah-choo!"*

"And that's another thing," B said. "When you

sneeze, nothing happens. With everyone else who's sick, the sneezes cause magical mishaps."

"Only until their magic runs out," Mayor Cumberland said, wagging a finger in B's face. "Don't forget, I know a thing or two about health!"

"Right," B said. "But if your magic is gone, then how did you transport here? And you were just about to transport back!"

Mayor Cumberland took a step away from the group. "No, I wasn't. I . . . I keep forgetting that my magic's gone. As for getting here, my, er, my wife did the spell."

B could tell from the looks on Madame Mel's and Mr. Bishop's faces that they weren't buying Mayor Cumberland's excuses. Still, technically, what he said was possible. There had to be some way to prove he still had magic! But what?

"Are you done?" the mayor asked crossly. "This has wasted too much of my precious time."

B had a flash of an idea. "Then go home," she said.

Mayor Cumberland's disgust for B was written plain across his face. "I would, know-it-all, if I were able to rhyme!" He blinked. "Chime, dime, lime, time, climb, prime, slime . . ."

"What's happening?" Trina cried.

"I tricked him into rhyming!" B yelled. " 'Time' and 'rhyme' — he accidentally made a spell! And now he's stuck saying rhyming words until the spell fades. He's got his magic, all right! He never ate the chocolate because he knew better. He's the poisoner!"

"Mime, grime, crime, sublime," said the horrified mayor, who finally clapped his hands over his mouth.

Madame Mel took out her Crystal Ballphone and pressed a button. In a few seconds her Dismantle Squad assembled itself magically beside her.

At the sight of the burly witches, Mayor Cumblerland wailed. "No need for them, no need! I confess. I did put a potion into the chocolate. Oh dear, oh dear, oh dear!"

"But why?" B's dad said. "Why on earth would you sabotage our products?"

The mayor cringed. "I . . . it . . . I was only trying to help," he said. "As head of health for the M.R.S., I tried to think what I could do to help witches stay healthier. The number of witches who overindulge on chocolate is staggering! Simply staggering. So when you invited me to come as mayor to the dipping debut, I thought, here's a chance to teach witches not to eat so much chocolate."

"By taking away their magic?" B said. "You're the head of *health*! You're not supposed to give people a terrible disease!"

By now the mayor was wringing his spotted red handkerchief between his hands. "I never meant to hurt anyone, I swear," he said. "The potion was only meant to give witches purple spots. Then people would stop eating the chocolate. I never, never wanted to make people so sick that they lost their powers."

"You could have ruined our business," Mr. Cicely said. "We employ hundreds of witches here at Enchanted Chocolates."

Mayor Cumblerland sniffed. "Why don't you start selling dehydrated turnip crisps? They're really quite delicious, once you get used to them."

Mr. Bishop stifled a laugh. Madame Mel whispered to her Dismantle Squad, and they silently transported elsewhere.

"Did you put the same potion in the chocolate today, Wallace?" Madame Mel said.

"Heavens no!" The mayor wiped his sweating face with the handkerchief. "I made a potion to reverse the effects of the first one. I hope. That's what I put in today's chocolate."

"As if any sickened witches would eat Fabulous Fruits now," B muttered.

"An excellent point," Madame Mel said. "Wallace, tell me what you put in these potions. Then we can finally get to the bottom of this mess."

She and the mayor conferred for a few minutes, during which time George, who had climbed back out of the chocolate, did a miniature victory dance.

"It's all settled," Madame Mel announced. "Wallace has explained to me the ingredients he used in his first potion. I'll be able to brew an antidote and get the witches who were sickened by the first potion back up on their feet."

Mayor Cumberland gave a weak smile to everyone in the room.

"And," Madame Mel went on, "Wallace agrees that his mayoral duties get in the way of his post as head of health. He'll be taking an immediate retirement from his M.R.S. position."

It was all B could do not to cheer.

Chapter 18

Mayor Cumberland transported himself off in disgrace, with no further mention of the many important meetings he'd missed, and everyone left in the room sighed with relief.

"I never voted for him, I'll have you know," B's dad said. "Two vats of chocolate wasted! Who does he think he is, poisoning my chocolate? Twice!"

"It's all behind you now," Madame Mel said. "Thank goodness."

"It wouldn't be if it weren't for B," Mr. Cicely said, ruffling B's hair. "Excellent work!"

Madame Mel turned to Mr. Bishop. "It seems I owe you an apology."

Mr. Bishop laughed. "Think nothing of it."

Finally B got the confidence to ask about

something she'd been dying to know. "What did you do, Mr. Bishop, to make Madame Mel suspect you?"

Her magical tutor's dark eyes twinkled. "When I was about your age, B, Madame Mel was my tutor. A much stricter one than I am to you, I daresay. One week, she told me I was going to have a quiz on Friday. The week came and went, and I didn't study like I should, but I had learned how to make a tummy ache potion. So I slipped it to Madame Mel in a piece of her favorite chocolate, to get out of the quiz."

"His potion was so potent, I was on the couch for a week," Madame Mel said. "Needless to say, I still failed him on that quiz."

Mr. Bishop seemed to be struggling to keep a straight face. "It was very wrong, what I did, B," he said, "and I wouldn't want you getting any ideas." He patted his belly protectively.

"I wouldn't poison you!" B said with a grin. "Just who do you think I am?"

"A very clever young witch, who has just gotten me out of a spot of trouble," Mr. Bishop replied. "Thanks, B, for believing in me."

"I'm sorry that I didn't," Madame Mel said. "Forgive me for suspecting you, Doug."

He held up a hand. "Say no more."

"I insist you let me buy you a hot chocolate, to make it up to you," Madame Mel said. "I know a wonderful new place that's just opened up." And, arm in arm, the former student and his former teacher transported elsewhere.

B's dad watched them leave. His toes started tapping, his fingers twitching. "There's so much to do!" he cried. "We're going to relaunch Fabulous Fruits, bigger and better than before. I think I've found a better fruit supplier than Jameson's company. We're going to do a big splashy nationwide ad campaign — oh! Trina! I forgot to tell you. I've worked out a promotional deal with your manager. It's all set. You're going to sing the jingle on national TV!"

Trina grinned. "Fabulicious," she said. "I can't wait."

B's dad snapped his fingers. "And George. B, I'm sorry George couldn't be here, but you can see why that was necessary. But give him this for me, will you?" He pulled a package out of his pocket and handed it to B.

"What's in here?" she asked.

"Samples, from the testing kitchens, of the new candy bar he suggested," B's dad said. "The one with the cracker and the peanut brittle? I want him to be the first to try it. I think it's a winner. And I'm thinking we should break from our usual naming convention and call it the George Bar. What do you think?"

"I think George will be thrilled," B said, as loudly as she could, so that George's mouse-size whoops of joy wouldn't be audible.

A chime sounded from inside B's dad's pockets. It was his Crystal Ballphone ringing.

"Excuse me, ladies," he said, "but I need to take this. So much to do!" And he took off down the hall, leaving B and Trina alone in the Fabulous Fruits room.

"Hey! What about me!" said a tiny voice.

They scooped a very chocolaty George out of the mixing vat and set him on a paper towel.

"Bravo, George," B said. "We couldn't have done it without you."

"I wouldn't have been here at all, much less seen what happened, if you hadn't agreed to shrink me," George said.

"It took all three of us to crack this case," B said. "We make a great team."

"Absolutely," Trina said.

George said, "No question."

"Ready, George, to be your old size again?" B asked.

"I guess so," he said, "though being mouse-size has its advantages."

"In that case, you're too small to sample the George Bar," Trina teased.

"Make me big this minute!" George squeaked.

"R-E-T-U-R-N," B spelled, laughing, and George resumed his normal size. But he was still covered head to foot in creamy, if tainted, milk chocolate.

"I've got an idea for a new Enchanted Chocolates candy," B said. "Chocolate-covered George!"

B's charmed adventures continue in
B Magical #6: The Superstar Sister

A loud drumbeat rattled through the kitchen ceiling, shaking the hanging lamps. B recognized the intro to "Swagger," a recent single from the Black Cats, her favorite band.

B pointed at the ceiling. "What's up?"

"It's your sister," her mom said. "She's been in her room ever since she got home from school, practicing her act for the school talent show. Have *you* done any practicing for your performance in the Young Witch Competition?"

B's spirits drooped. "I haven't gotten far. I can't make up my mind about what to do, or wear, or anything."

"Oh, there are so many possibilities," B's mom began. "I have an issue of *Spellbound Monthly* somewhere that had the cutest pictures for costumes. . . ."

A magazine full of adorable, complicated costumes was the last thing B wanted. "Mr. Bishop says he'll help me and Trina prepare."

"He can really help you out," B's mom said.

"Help who out with what?" Mr. Cicely appeared in the doorway and set down his laptop bag.

"We were just discussing Friday's Young Witch Competition," Mrs. Cicely said.

He sat down. "She'll clobber everyone else. It runs in the family."

"Now, Felix," B's mom said. "B isn't going to 'clobber' anyone. So as long as she works hard and does her best, she'll have nothing to fear."

Upstairs Dawn's fancy footwork thumped. "Do

your best" scarcely seemed like enough when your older sister was overloaded with both talent and magical skill.

"Dawn, come for dinner," B's mom called up the stairs. "Dawn! Dawn! Oh, never mind. There's no stopping her practicing."

B swallowed a mouthful of dinner. Her mom's magical cooking was always delicious, but this time B couldn't taste a thing. It was bad enough having to demonstrate her magical skills to an audience and panel of judges. That was enough stage fright to render her clumsy and speechless for a week. But living up to Dawn was impossible, plain and simple.

"Why the long face, B?" her dad said.

"Oh, nothing," B said. "Pass the nachos, please."